TICK TOCK

To Gail –
An inspiring woman
you are and a great role-
model!

Seth Schapira

TICK TOCK

Lillian Schapiro

iUniverse, Inc.
New York Lincoln Shanghai

TICK TOCK

iUniverse books may be ordered through booksellers or by contacting:

iUniverse
2021 Pine Lake Road, Suite 100
Lincoln, NE 68512
www.iuniverse.com
1-800-Authors (1-800-288-4677)

This is a work of fiction. Any similarity of characters to actual people is purely coincidental.

ISBN-13: 978-0-595-36265-3 (pbk)
ISBN-13: 978-0-595-80710-9 (ebk)
ISBN-10: 0-595-36265-6 (pbk)
ISBN-10: 0-595-80710-0 (ebk)

Printed in the United States of America

Dedicated to my wonderful husband, who helped me see the humor when I thought life was too unfair to be funny.

Thanks to my parents, and to my editor, Sandra Pourciau. Their confidence inspired me to persevere.

CHAPTER 1

▼

BEING SMART DOESN'T
STOP THE CLOCK

It's a prerequisite for infertility that your best friends got pregnant just by looking at their husbands, not just one of your best friends, but two. And, it comes up all the time. You're talking about the once a year sale at Neiman Marcus and somehow, this reminds her of getting pregnant on the first try. Not just once, not just twice, but three times. Two of your best friends. Three pregnancies each. Just from talking, almost. Maybe she got pregnant after the Neiman Marcus sale; just the sheer exhilaration of having saved hundreds of dollars in one afternoon made that egg gobble up that sperm. Which designer was it? Dana Buchman? Albert Nipon? Even if it's not on sale, that designer outfit, including the matching shoes, purse, and earrings was certainly cheaper and less painful than the whole infertility scene. You get a little superstitious after a while.

But, both of my fertile friends are teeny tiny, even after having their children. Neither of them look like hearty, peasant breeding stock. One wears a Banana Republic size 0 and the other an Anne Taylor 4. The size 0 works out at least once a day, has a high power corporate job, would describe herself as "very intense," and not an ounce of fat on her—all the prerequisites for infertility. Anne Taylor 4 never has a strand of her beautiful, straight black hair out of place, never has even a hint of a zit on her skin, never has stray papers on her desk, never loses her temper, and, even after three children, was featured, in full color, on the cover of her corporate magazine. How can they be fertile?

My mother, a tall, robust woman, got pregnant with me on the first try. I don't know when she told me this devastating information, but she did. It might have been when I told her about my freak uterus. I remember standing at some public place, maybe the grocery store, on a pay phone, trying to explain some portion of my infertility, and she told me that she got pregnant on the first try. Once again, despite an Ivy League education, medical school and residency, I did not quite measure up; something was missing, I was not quite good enough.

My mother has always been a symbol of strength, a sturdy frame with wide hips, that, until I wanted to be pregnant, I had always been glad not to have. Sales people, cashiers and new acquaintances can't wait to tell us how alike we look. We are both about 5 feet, seven inches tall with prominent (let's not say large) noses, freckles which get darker in the summer, and wavy, brown hair. I've never thought of myself as a brunette. To me, a brunette has long, flowing hair, like the girl on the L'Oreal box, and has nothing in common with me and my wash and wear brown hair. As long as I can remember, Mom has always had short wavy hair. As I watched her auburn highlights turn gray, I determined that that would never happen to me. My hair will remain forever long and brown with auburn highlights. Once, a brave hair dresser tried to straighten it. After applying some very expensive blue gel, she worked and worked with her straightening iron until the salon closed. Since I do not have that kind of time in my life, my hair remains wavy, with what I like to call a "natural perm." The brown hair with auburn highlights would showcase our empathetic hazel eyes, green with gray in the middle, except that we both keep our eyes hidden behind glasses. I replace my eye glasses every two years, and she every four or five years, so we share a slightly out of date look. I am an Anne Taylor size 6, Talbots size 4, version of my mother.

Note that I did not say my parents got pregnant, but my mother got pregnant. Women get pregnant. Men do not. Women get the bloody news first; there you are, alone in the bathroom, staring at the blood on the toilet paper, maybe tormented by a few cramps, undeniably not pregnant, no baby, just a period, again. The cramps and the bloody mess increase, conspiring to rub in your face the fact that you failed, again. And, you know that you are failing where your mother clearly succeeded, or you would not be here to fail.

When I was not pregnant the first month, I knew that I would need the most expensive, most complicated procedures out there. My husband, Steven, a man who feels most comfortable in a Brooks Brothers blue blazer and, at almost six feet tall with full brown hair and deep brown eyes, looks like a model for the Ivy

League school where we met, and I were not good at saving money. We tried, once. Trying our luck on a discount vacation, we flew on People's Express airline, rented a 2-door hatchback from "Rent a Wreck," and stayed at some cheap motel with its own mini-golf course. By the time we finished buying our own meals for the plane, buying all the insurance offered from the car agency and buying clean, soft sheets and a warmer, unstained comforter for the motel, we could have flown first class on United Airlines, driven around in a full-size, four-door sedan, or maybe even a Town Car, from Hertz or Avis, and stayed at a Four Seasons. We are not the types who are successfully frugal, and I knew right away that pregnancy would not be any different.

At the time, I was too busy to keep a diary, so some of the details of other people, may not be totally correct. Some, I have changed completely. What happened to me, however, every emotion and every medical instrument grabbing my pelvic organs, I remember exactly.

When my blasted period appeared exactly fourteen days after our first carefully timed attempt at conception, I started keeping a basal body temperature chart. I have never been able to read those mercury thermometers and I hoped that a digital one would be accurate enough. Every morning, before you move, before you kiss your husband, and certainly before you get up to go to the bathroom, you reach over to the night stand, moving as little as possible so that you did not disturb your basal body temperature, grope around for the thermometer, and pop it under your tongue, all to try to tell when you are ovulating. If the thermometer falls on the floor and you reach down to pick it up, that fouls up the results and you will not be able to tell if you ovulated or just hyperventilated that month. You are looking for a dip, followed the next day by a blip. Once the dip and the blip appear on the graph, it's time for, "Okay, honey, today's the day." The final result should be a jagged graph with a small dip followed by a spike, and then a plateau, like a good stock, if you buy at the dip. Of course, despite my nice 28 day cycles, my temperature chart was flat. Flat as a pancake. Flat as Iowa. Flat as my non-pregnant belly. No ups, no downs, no good time to buy the stock. After two months of the annoying, and flat, basal body temperature chart, I told Steven that I was not ovulating (just what every husband wants to hear at 5:30 in the morning), and that I needed to take Clomid, the dreaded fertility pill.

"Amy, please, get a real doctor's opinion," he replied light heartedly. "Last I heard, Dr. Amy Levine was still in training." Steven was a great guy; his eyes showed his deep compassion for others and his calves showed his years of tennis at boarding school. Without knowing his great sense of humor or patience, but perhaps sensing them from his presence, I had fallen in love with him at first site, in the common room outside the college dining hall. The room was wood paneled, with the fall setting sun streaming in through stained glass windows. He had been resting comfortably on a slightly worn green velvet couch, wearing a polo shirt, khaki slacks, and penny loafers with pennies in the loafers, but no socks. One of our first dates had been "borrowing" trays from the dining hall and using them to sled down the steep, snowy hill behind the Divinity School. Although I could often convince him to go along with, what he considered, my zany ideas, he had insisted that we wait to get married and to have children until we were a bit settled, or at least out of school and earning some money. He did not seem terribly concerned that I was not pregnant after one or two attempts, but he was, in general, more patient than I.

Granted, I was only a third year resident in OB/GYN, but I was doing my second infertility rotation and, in my mind, that made me an expert. It also made it easy for me to see not just a "real doctor," but a specialist. That afternoon, after lecture, I asked my attending physician, Dr. Taylor, if he had a minute. He was definitely one of the best looking attendings, tall with graying hair and blue eyes with a comforting sparkle. A former Duke basketball player, he carried his tall figure gracefully, always in a tailored suit unless he was in the operating room. Even in his green hospital scrubs, he maintained an air of elegance. To my surprise, instead of just a quick chat in the hall, he invited me into his office. It was a university office, fluorescent lights, mostly white tile floors and white walls. Since he had recently moved, there was no rug on the floor, but there was a picture of his family on the desk, a pretty, blond wife and three smiling, blond boys that looked about 4, 6 and 8 years old. They were sitting outside of a tent, apparently quite cheerful about the rainfall the night before. I remember that he sat in a spacious, leather reclining chair, behind a large, wooden, doctor-like desk. The image is clear in my mind, although I don't remember the exact conversation.

After sitting down in a bare metal chair that appeared to have been taken from a classroom, I presented him with my temperature chart and told him that I thought I needed a prescription for Clomid because I was not ovulating. What could he say? The chart looked exactly like the anovulatory (not ovulating) chart from the lecture he had given us the week before, except the patient for the model chart had marked when she had had sex with a green X on certain dates. Trying to maintain a bit of privacy, I didn't want Dr. Taylor to know whether we had a wild and crazy sex life, jumping between the sheets eager for each other at the end of every day, or whether I collapsed from exhaustion at the end of a day which started at 5 a.m. and Steven usually found me asleep in front of the refrigerator, a half empty bowl of spaghetti in my hand.

Despite the lack of green X's, Dr. Taylor agreed that my ovaries had not done their thing those two months. He pulled a small, rectangular pad of white papers out of his pocket and scribbled out a prescription for me. "Clomid can make you irritable, Amy" he said with laugh. "You'd better warn your husband."

I can't remember if I had any blood work done first, or if I just took the Clomid. I always have my patients get some tests done first, but I did not have time for that. When I did not get pregnant after the first month, I stopped him in the hallway and he gave me a prescription for a higher dose.

My mother, a physician, but not a gynecologist, weighed in with her opinion: the drug had to be dangerous. "Causing irritability," made it a mood altering drug, and she reminded me of the patients I had seen during my psychiatry rotation who had recurrent psychotic episodes throughout their lives from having experimented with PCP. The first month that I took Clomid, the New England Journal published an article linking Clomid with ovarian cancer. Mom called me the day before the Clomid and ovarian cancer article came out, predicting that Clomid must cause ovarian cancer because it stimulated your ovaries. Fortunately, we had already discussed it in our weekly journal review, so I explained that not having babies was associated with ovarian cancer, and that if I could get pregnant, I could then leave that high risk group. I would rather be part of the Clomid group than the childless group, since I seemed destined to be in at least one of the groups. As it turned out in the article, only women who had taken more than 12 months of Clomid had an increased risk of ovarian cancer. Before I even had a chance to fill my first prescription, I reassured my mother that I would not take more than 12 months of Clomid.

During the months that I took the Clomid, I used ovulation predictor kits instead of recording a basal body temperature chart. Today, you just have to pee on the end of a stick. Back then, you needed a PhD in chemistry to figure out how to use those kits. There were lots of little pieces and lots of little steps. You had to pee into the cup, then remove several drops with a dropper, put them in a cup, then add three drops from bottle A, wait three minutes, then add two drops from bottle B, wait another three minutes, then pour the concoction onto a disc and wait two minutes. I woke up at 4:30 a.m. to do this, because it was not supposed to be from the first time you emptied your bladder in the morning. You had to get up, pee, wait until you had to pee again, then do this entire science experiment, then make love with enough time left to stay lying down with a pillow under your bottom for 20 minutes, before getting to work on time.

Needless to say, the second month did not work either.

My next visit with Dr. Taylor was another a hallway consultation, standing in the fluorescent lighting of the hallway, in front of a patient's half-open door. I did not want to bother him and take up too much of his time, although worrying about getting pregnant took up almost all of my waking and sleeping hours. Being on the fertility rotation, work was certainly no escape, dealing with other people's problems getting pregnant. As a tall, good-looking man with a very easy manner Dr. Taylor was the doctor that everyone picked to "just ask a question," which means an informal consultation, which could take quite a while.

After the second month taking Clomid ended in a period instead of a pregnancy, I told him that I thought that I needed a hysterosalpingogram. A hysterosalpingogram, usually referred to as an HSG, tested the uterus and fallopian tubes. It is done in the radiology department, with a doctor, usually your gynecologist, putting in a speculum, and then inserting a thin rubber tube into the uterus. A radiologist and a technician are also in the room, to ensure complete lack of privacy. Speculum exams were never my favorite, but the most painful part comes when the balloon at the end of the tube is inflated to secure it into the uterus. Sometimes, the doctor needs to grasp the end of the uterus, called the cervix, with a vicious piece of metal equipment called a tenaculum. Aptly called a single tooth tenaculum, the tenaculum has one sharp "tooth" at either end, designed to pierce the cervix, so that the doctor can hold onto it. Having had my cervix grasped on more than one occasion with a tenaculum, I can tell you that it doesn't feel good, but isn't as bad as you might imagine. The uterus translates the sensation into cramping, so you just have the sensation of having a period with a speculum stuck inside of you.

Dr. Taylor encouraged me to try one more month of Clomid, telling me that HSG's were not a lot of fun. No, I insisted, I wanted one.

CHAPTER 2

▼

LUNCH HOUR

With Dr. Taylor's permission, I scheduled my HSG. It had to be during lunch, between my morning and afternoon clinics. When the day arrived, I finished my morning clinic and raced down to the radiology department. Dr. Taylor was waiting for me, wearing hospital scrubs, having worked me in between cases on his operating day. As he told me where to go to change into a lovely hospital gown, I worried that I was making him late for his next surgery. If I remember correctly, the hospital gown was the classic white with blue fleur-de-lis pattern, open in the back, no matter how tightly you tied it. When I emerged from the changing room, holding the back of the gown closed with a hand behind my back, Dr. Taylor gently instructed me to lie on the coffin-thin radiology table and to place my feet in a frog-leg position.

The few times that I had done HSG's on my patients, I had been so focused on actually doing the procedure and finding out the results that I had never noticed how completely undignified the entire process was. As I lay on the table in my thin, little gown, staring up at the overpowering fluoroscopy machine, I felt at once dwarfed by the equipment but gigantically exposed in this position.

I winced as Dr. Taylor slipped the ice cold speculum between my legs. Thank goodness, I had remembered to shave my legs that morning. Next, a thin, rubber catheter, that looked quite innocent, was inserted into my cervix. At the end of the innocent-looking catheter was a balloon. When that balloon was inflated, it felt, just as I had told my patients, like a horrible menstrual cramp. Only this felt worse than what I had described to my patients. The cramp just stayed, and I could not roll up in a ball or take Motrin, like I did when I had my period. We waited while the technician called the radiologist. After three minutes, (I was watching the clock) of cramping eternity, the radiologist strolled in. From my position on the table, I could hear his voice and see the bright red, lead gown he wore to protect himself from the rays he would be shooting into my ovaries, but I could not see his face. He was just a voice emanating from a lead gown.

The radiologist, who must have introduced himself, but I don't remember, instructed Dr. Taylor, whom he called Jim, to inject the dye. As they injected dye into my uterus and beamed X-Rays at my reproductive organs, I twisted my head to see a corner of the results on the television monitor. As Dr. Taylor injected the dye into my uterus, which caused more cramping, he asked if I remembered Stacey, a vivacious brunette with a taut soccer body, a friend and fellow obstetrics resident who had left the program two years ago. I tried hard to focus on his voice, which was almost drowned out by the screaming cramps from my uterus. He told me that Stacey had just died of breast cancer at age 32, leaving behind her husband and a three month old son. Stacey had been a wonderful, vivacious person, with a great sense of humour, dancing brown eyes and brunette hair, like the lady on the L'Oreal box. Even a long night on call did not dim the light in her eyes or the flow of her brunette locks. I remember her joking, in her hospital bed just hours after her mastectomy, that her hair and her breasts were her most treasured possessions and now she would lose them both.

That was before she had her son. As I lay on the table with my knees bent and my feet in stirrups in the required gynecology position, Dr. Taylor told me that, before she died, Stacey had made a videotape for her son, reading children's stories and singing him lullabies. I pictured Stacey with the flowing hair that she had before the chemotherapy. Tears welled up in my eyes; I missed Stacey. Would I rather have a child than my life? No one had asked her. What would she have chosen? At least she had had a few months to enjoy her baby boy.

The severe cramp of the inflation of the balloon inside of my uterus brought me back to the matter at hand. Craning my neck to the side, I studied the monitor with the picture of dye filling my uterus. Oh, shit. That was not a normal uterus. It was from the textbook of freak uteruses. After the cervix, the dye went into two divided cavities. The good news was that the tubes were open. The "tubes," properly called the fallopian tubes, transported the eggs from the ovary and were the meeting ground for the egg and sperm.

As soon as the procedure was over, I slowly sat up on the table and then walked back to the dressing room, holding the back of my gown closed in an attempt to cover my body and to shield myself from any more bad news. After pulling back on my undies, pantyhose, blue sheath dress and black flat pump shoes, I readjusted my pony tail and left the tiny dressing cubicle to meet Dr. Taylor in the radiology viewing room. He had Tim, one of the junior residents, with him looking at *my* HSG. Tim was actually one of my favorite residents, a hard worker, understanding with the patients, calm under pressure, a sure hand in the operating room, and always ready with a joke at any resident gathering. Six feet two, a former college football player with deep blue eyes and brown hair, Tim did not need to share my secrets to win popularity. He was the only junior resident not to look foolish in the short white jacket.

"I hope you don't mind," Dr. Taylor said, his gentle voice making it almost okay. "I'm just using it as a teaching tool." Talk about feeling violated. Here was a guy that I work with, who was supposed to be my junior, looking inside my uterus, and not a very good looking uterus at that. I tried to be "mature," if that was the right word.

"Not at all, but let's keep this confidential," I managed to say, fighting back tears. Like anything was confidential in a small residency training program where people share life-altering experiences on a daily basis and routinely work 36 hours or more together at a stretch.

But, Tim could not hide the excitement in his eyes, excited about some actual pathology, not just from a text-book, but right up there on the X-Ray box. All in all, it really did not make my day any worse: friend's tragic death raising questions about justice in the world, freak uterus potentially meaning that I can never carry a child. Why not throw in a little invasion of privacy?

Dr. Taylor, Tim and I stood in front of the X-ray, the black and white image hanging in front of the glaring light box. Although he pretended to be teaching the junior resident, I knew that Dr. Taylor was talking to me. With his finger, he traced the abnormal outline of my uterus; instead of a nice, neat, almost isosceles triangle, there were two crazy rabbit ears. "This could be a bicornuate or a septate uterus. If it's a septum, it looks pretty thick. We can do a laparoscopy to find out," he said.

I had not only seen more than I wanted to see, I did not think that I could stand in front of that view box with Tim and Dr. Taylor, two really good looking guys, both with fertile wives, having an academic discussion about *my* uterine anomaly, for one more second.

"Well, I'm late for clinic. I've gotta run," I said, excusing myself, and headed into the winding corridors of the radiology department. It took what seemed like forever to find my way back to the main hospital, each corridor having more corners than I remembered, the fluorescent light buzzing overhead, like bees gossiping about my HSG, and then, through an underground tunnel, to reach the hospital exit. The bright sun struck my eyes sharply after the darkness of the radiology department. I could not believe that it was a beautiful, sunny day.

As I waited for the newly painted shuttle bus with its bold italic letters to take me to the clinic building, I tried to focus on the cheerfulness of the sun and the beautiful clear blue sky. The sun light really seemed quite harsh to me. I hoped that I did not start sweating under the rayon lining of my blue cotton dress. Fortunately, my white coat, embroidered with my name, Dr. Amy Levine, and my department, Obstetrics and Gynecology in elegant blue script letters, would hide any sweat stains. As a chief resident, I got to wear a long, white coat, not one of the short, goofy jackets.

Once inside the shuttle, however, I stared hard out of the window, trying to decide whether I was more upset about Stacey dying or about my hopes for a family dying. I could have cried for a few hours over either, or both. But, it was a short ride to clinic and the shuttle was full. In fact, someone was sitting next to me. "Nice weather we're having," I heard. "Yes, I hope it lasts," I managed to answer, still staring out the window. Missing lunch didn't even cross my mind.

Somehow, at clinic, I managed to focus on my patients. To add insult to injury, that afternoon had to be the obstetric clinic. The clinic was held in a new building, the outside bricks still clean and red, and the walls inside a joyful, periwinkle blue. The floors were still clean, white and bright. The receptionist, a middle aged, heavy-set woman, who had watched many generations of residents come and go, greeted me from behind her periwinkle blue counter, "Good afternoon, Doctor Levine. It's a busy one today."

"Thanks for the warning," I laughed, hoping she could not see the tears in the corners of my eyes behind my glasses.

I looked down the cheerful, periwinkle blue hallway. Four doors were closed and had charts in their clear plastic chart holders. I glanced at a few of the charts before picking a door to enter.

"Good afternoon, I'm Dr. Levine," I said brightly, as I entered the room, somehow putting the events before the shuttle ride into another compartment of my brain.

The patient, Shannon, was already sitting on the exam table, kicking her legs like a child on a stool whose legs did not reach the floor. She was probably only five feet tall, a bit chubby, with short blond hair, a few pimples on her forehead, but an innocent looking face around her crooked teeth, which were as stained from tobacco as a fifteen year old's can be. Her blue jean shorts appeared to have been cut off from long blue jeans, cut a bit long for shorts, coming just above the knee, with the edges still frayed. Her T-shirt had remains of a faded bunny rabbit decal that looked like an Easter T-shirt bought on sale after the holiday. Bright pink nails with white polka dots stood boldly in her worn, yellow, plastic flip-flops. She did not respond and continued kicking her legs and staring at the tile floor. I followed her gaze. All I saw was a clean tile floor, white with black streaks with no particular pattern.

Looking at her chart, I found out that she was fifteen years old and that this was her first pregnancy. "How are you today?" I asked.

She responded with a soft grunt.

I asked if she was in school.

She shook her head, indicating "no." (This was her first pregnancy, so it was conceivable that she still went to school.)

"Oh, do you have a job?" I asked.

"No," was her sullen, teenage response. At least, I had encouraged her to speak, even if it was only one syllable.

"Well, let's listen to the baby and see how it's growing," I continued, forcing good spirit into my voice. I took a tape measure from the table and measured her growing, pregnant belly. "24 centimeters. Excellent. That's exactly what it's supposed to be. Now, we'll listen to the baby's heart beat."

I squeezed some pale blue gel onto her belly and put the smooth, black head of the Doppler ultrasound on that spot. The fetal heart beat always sounded like a stampede of horses to me. "Sounds good," I offered.

"So, what do you do all day?" I asked, actually quite interested to find out what you do all day when you're fifteen, not in school, not working, and not on drugs. Her earlier drug tests had been negative.

"Uh unh uh," she intoned, implying that she did not know either.

I asked how she was feeling with her pregnancy. "Unhn."

I pulled the wheeled doctor stool in front of her swinging legs and sat down, trying to catch her gaze.

"Is there anything you'd like to talk about?"

"Mmhmm."

"Do you go to one of the schools that has daycare at the school?" I inquired, genuinely concerned.

Shoulder shrug for response.

"Well, I'd like you to see the social worker before you leave today. Will you do that?"

She nodded in a way I hoped could be properly interpreted as a yes.

I put a note on her chart for the nurse to send her to the social worker.

"We will see you back in two weeks," I said, just before leaving the room. The normal routine would not have required her to come back for four weeks, but we liked to monitor the teenagers more closely and give them more support.

Picking the next chart out of the box, I read that Arlene was sixteen, this was her second pregnancy, marked as high risk with yellow highlighted circles around risk factors of age and closely spaced pregnancies. Apparently, neither the contraception talk before her discharge, nor the prescription for birth control pills after the last baby's delivery had been terribly successful. I plunged in and did my best, but met with little more success than I had with Shannon. Even asking questions about her baby at home elicited nothing more than a teenage shrug, and a few words about her grandma watching the baby.

I remembered the next patient, Sandy, from her last pregnancy, just a few months before. She was what we called a brittle diabetic. Although she had been diabetic for twelve years, since age 11, she did not follow her diet or take her insulin. One of her problems from the diabetes included slow gut activity, so she was already quite thin before pregnancy. She wore thick glasses from diabetic retinopathy and had an amazingly devil-may-care attitude about the whole thing. Her thick, brown hair was always matted along her back, making me wish that I had an extra half an hour to gently weed out the knots. She had been hospitalized for most of her last pregnancy, partly because she had no phone to call us with her sugars and partly because it was difficult for her to get a ride to the hospital for her appointments, so she missed several months of appointments when she was feeling well. The entire first two months, she had been in the hospital due to severe morning sickness, called hyperemesis gravidarum. We had a devil of a time keeping her sugars from getting too low or too high. Both were dangerous. Then, around 26 weeks, she had developed toxemia of pregnancy, severe preeclampsia. With strict hospital bed rest, monitoring her kidney function and the baby's growth and placental blood flow daily, she made it to 29 weeks and then had to be delivered because her kidney function deteriorated so badly. No one came to visit her until the baby was born. But, here she was, six months later, Fertile Myrtle, back for more. By the way, that first baby, so far, was doing well.

So, why couldn't I get pregnant?

CHAPTER 3

▼

THE MORNING SPECIMEN

After clinic, I went to the library to do some research on my freak uterus. I had been on call and not slept at all the night before, but I could stave off sleep a little longer. The buzzing of the florescent library lights, the humming of the computer, and the flickering of the green letters on the computer screen bore into my throbbing head. But, I forced my eyes to focus. That night, I went home with an armload of articles and several books on bicornuate and septate uteruses.

Steven was already at the apartment, waiting for me. Sweetheart that he was, he had picked up my favorite dinner, sushi.

We lived in a one bedroom apartment on the second floor of a two story apartment complex, built on the motel model, with olive green window treatments, and yellowing shades pulled down in front of most of the windows. There was no elevator, which made moving in a challenge, but made us feel better about not having a lot of "stuff." We still lived, basically, like students. The living room/dining room area had the faded, brown couch from college where we'd had our first kiss, a television set and a plain faux-wood fiberboard dining room table with four matching chairs. The kitchen consisted of a refrigerator, oven, two-burner electric stove, a small amount of counter space and some cabinets above. In the bedroom, we had a King-size mattress on a metal frame on coasters, a maroon bedspread hanging down to the old brown carpeted floor, and a scratched, wooden chest of drawers missing a few strategic handles.

We sat cross-legged on the bed, divided the articles into two piles, poured a thin layer of soy sauce on top of the sushi so that we would not have to look up too often, and started reading.

There really was not that much written on the subject of "uterine anomalies" or freak uteruses. Most of the textbooks had barely a paragraph on each anomaly.

A uterine septum was not that big of a deal. The articles claimed that a septum could cause repetitive miscarriages, but not infertility. A septum could be taken care of with outpatient surgery. I knew all of that.

A bicornuate uterus, on the other hand, was a big deal. Your uterus had two "horns," just like the devil. In some circumstances, neither of them could support a pregnancy. There was a fancy procedure to attempt to reconstruct a normal uterus, but this might also tear apart during the course of a pregnancy, potentially killing both baby and mother. Or, the uterus could be so scarred from the surgical procedure for the correction of the anomaly that you could not get pregnant at all. It seemed clear that most of the articles about reconstructing the uterus were from one specialist. If we decided to do that, if that's what I had, then we'd go to him. Good, that much was settled.

But what did I have? Only I could have a freak uterus that was so freaky that an HSG could not tell us what it was. Between bites of sushi, I read that for diagnosis of the condition, you could either have a surgery, the laparoscopy Dr. Taylor had talked about earlier, or just have a fancy X-Ray called an MRI to distinguish between a bicornuate or a septate uterus. Well, I certainly did not want to have surgery and miss work if I did not have to.

Dr. Taylor was leaning toward doing a laparoscopy first, but I did not want *him* to do the procedure to reconstruct the bicornuate uterus into a regular uterus, if that's what I had. I wanted the expert who had written all of the articles to do my surgery if I had a bicornuate uterus. Then I would not need a laparoscopy; I would need a laparotomy, a much bigger deal, a C-Section style incision that would put me out of work for about six weeks. If I were out for that long, I would have to repeat an entire year of residency.

Steven and I looked at each other over the pile of articles, and over the now empty sushi cartons. I was too tired to cry; I had put it off for too long. I looked at his kind brown eyes. Was he disappointed? Did he really care if we had children? We had talked about how many children we wanted, but we had never talked about not having the children we wanted. I stared at the ceiling as Steven collected the stack of articles and sushi containers. I watched his calves (he had great legs), as he walked out of the room. "What if I can't have children?" I wanted to ask. "Will you still love me? Will you still be my husband?" But, I did not dare say that; I did not want to know. He could certainly find some fertile woman; younger, cuter, and easier to live with than I.

"I need to watch some trash television," I said, instead.

"You must be wiped out. Did you get any sleep last night?" he asked.

"A minute here and there, between emergencies," I answered, wanting to tell him how much I had hated having gorgeous, football player Tim see my HSG, and how scared I was.

Before the first commercial, I was sound asleep. Steven gently woke me, just enough to guide my legs under the covers.

The alarm jarred me back to reality. A picture of my freak uterus, those clear, bright white horns against the black background on the X-Ray light box, filled my mind. The thought of surgery did not scare me, but never having children did. I reached over to Steven for a first and final snuggle, before throwing myself out of bed to start another day.

As Steven was pouring himself a bowl of cereal, I told him that, even though all the problems seemed to be on my side, (not ovulating, freak uterus), he should get tested too.

"Sure, honey," he said, easily. "What should I do?"

"A semen analysis."

"A what?"

"A semen analysis. I brought home a sterile cup. I can bring it back to the lab this morning."

Poor guy. He did not even get any magazines. (Don't worry. Less than a year later, we were at a fancy fertility clinic which lots of pornography magazines and plastic couches.)

"Right now?"

"It has to be fresh," I explained. "The little guys don't last very long in the cup. They have got to get right under the microscope. We can do it tomorrow, if you need some magazines or something."

"No, that's okay," Steven answered, still looking a bit perplexed. After eight years together, he was used to my lack of subtlety in most matters. Hazard of the profession. When the word "vagina" comes up at work many times every day or even every hour, you don't cringe at the words "semen" and "analysis." Well, you might, because that's the other side of things, the man side.

I finished pulling up my pantyhose. Everyone in this residency program dressed nicely for clinic. I would have rather worn scrubs and sneakers, but I donned a trim, forest green dress, a single strand of pearls and the flattest pumps that I had been able to find. I grabbed a granola bar and an apple to eat in the car on my way to the hospital and almost left without Steven's sample.

Steven had not reappeared yet, and I knew that this type of thing should be handled delicately. But, that was not my style. "Honey, do you need help?" I said to the closed door. I was not quite sure how I would help, but I was certain that I could come up with something. Frankly, I was a bit embarrassed by the whole process.

A hand emerged, simple, gold wedding band around the fourth finger, clean, neatly filed nails, holding the plastic cup.

"Do you want to come with me?" I asked. "The lab techs will probably let us look at it."

"That's okay. I think I've seen enough for one day," came the laughing voice from behind the cheap, wooden door.

"All right. Well, I'm off. I'll call if I get a minute. I love you." I said, as I headed out, making certain that the top of the once sterile cup was screwed on tightly, before dropping the clear, plastic specimen container into my purse. It would be ugly if that spilled. It's one thing to have a chocolate bar melt in your purse and get on your keys, but this...

I got into my ten year old, light blue Buick Skylark, a hand me down from my father, and was glad that the morning sun had not gotten too warm, yet. I did not want anything to have a bad effect on the little guys swimming in their cup in my purse. I turned on the air conditioner to be sure. The radio blasted country western music. I found country western music, the new rock version, to be quite the lifesaver. Even if you did not know the song, you could generally pick up the lyrics and sing along after the first refrain. My current favorite refrain was, "I like my women on the trashy side," by a group called The Confederate Railroad. Driving along with the wind blowing across my face and belting out country western music had probably saved my life on more than one occasion, keeping me awake as I drove home after a 36 or 37 hour work day.

There was not much traffic between our apartment and the hospital and, after two songs, one about decorating a double wide trailer and another about walking in on your man and your sister, I swung my Buick into the residents' parking area. When I turned off the car, the engine made a queer, grinding noise. Looking down, I realized that I had forgotten to shift into park. The gear shift would not move until I turned the engine back on, making another ominous grinding noise. This was not how I wanted this day to start; I needed some good news.

After properly parking the car and silently praying that I had not done any permanent damage to the transmission, I headed right to the lab and asked the cheerfully bright-eyed, white-coated technician if he could look at a semen analy-sis for me. The technician said that that test was done in a different lab, and he was not sure what time those technicians arrived in the morning.

Steven was not going to be happy with me if these little guys all died before the lab opened. I could hear him joking that he really preferred me to a little plas-tic cup, and asking if I was trying to tell him something. Hopefully, he preferred me to a little plastic cup. What if he didn't prefer me to a little plastic cup with a green lid? Where was my confidence? Of course, he preferred me to a little plastic cup, no matter what color the lid.

Fortunately, when I found the other laboratory in the maze of laboratories, the technicians were already going strong. "Sure, doc," another nice young man in a white lab coat said. "Do you want to stay and look? It will only take a minute."

"Yeh, thanks," I said. No reason to go into details. No reason to explain to this amiable and enthusiastic young man that this was my husband's sperm sample, that I had failed all of my fertility tests miserably, and that I may, in fact, be the most infertile person in the world.

In a few moments, the same, clean shaven young man with short, cropped brown hair and a prematurely receding hairline was sitting in front of a micro-scope, his head bent in concentration, looking at a slide of my husband's sperm. "This looks great," he said enthusiastically. "Come look at this," he continued, stepping away from the microscope so I could step in.

He explained to me that he looked at how many sperm there were, whether or not they swam, whether they swam straight, and how they were shaped. Well, it was quite clear that these perfectly shaped guys were swimming at top speed straight to Yale. Bright little suckers.

Well, that was good news. But, that meant that it was all *my* fault. Now, Steven could really just find some fertile young thing and start making babies; I was just in the way. How would I feel, I wondered, if things were reversed, if Steven had the problem, and I was perfect. Women always stood by their hus-bands; men left their wives when the wives were diagnosed with cancer, but I had never heard of a woman leaving her husband at a time like that. Many women have even taken back their exes to care for them through chemotherapy when the strains of real life turned out to be too much for that cute, young, lithe second wife. Driving an aging man to chemotherapy could interfere with tennis lessons and salon appointments, but the first wife, who had lost her figure bearing their children and driving them to their lessons, had time, once again, to be the care taker. I had not even had a chance to lose my figure having babies. All women worry about their husbands leaving them when they get old and fat, but I might not even last through the first round; the folds of fertility, bags of bearing babies might forever elude me, leaving me thin, wiry and alone.

The technician wrote up an official report for me to "put in the patient's file." I thanked him and headed out, not sure whether to be happy or sad. We did not both need to have problems, but did his have to be *so* perfect?! It was not fair. The whole thing was not fair.

I headed out of the main building and took the shuttle to the clinic. There was something soothing about the clinic. I think it was the hum of the air conditioner and the fact that, unlike the hospital, there was unlikely to be an absolute life-threatening emergency at any minute. Very few people "code," or have a cardiac arrest, at the gynecology clinic.

That morning's clinic was the endocrinology or infertility clinic. This was infertility clinic resident style. Most patients were there to discuss periods, or, more specifically, the lack thereof due to obesity, or they were patients from the state mental hospital who were on medication that made their breasts leak milk. The scene contrasted dramatically with the fertility clinic I would later attend, full of trim, professional women in suits, anxiously looking at their watches and worrying about being late for a meeting. The private practice, cash only, fertility clinic opened at 7 a.m., so that we could all be at work by 9, which was as late as most of us could arrange to start our busy work days. These women sat patiently, their assigned time being "morning," which started at 9 a.m.

Fortunately for me, Dr. Taylor was the attending in clinic that morning. He was wearing a trim, light grey suit that complimented his blue eyes. Over a light blue shirt, he wore a yellow tie with red squares, which seemed to me clearly to have been picked out by his wife. The resident would see a patient, leave the room, discuss the plan with the attending physician, and then return to the patient, sometimes with the attending. Obviously, there could be quite a wait to see the attending, since several residents were working in the clinic at one time.

Picking up the first chart, I opened the door. A large child, sixteen years old and 250 pounds, was sitting on the exam table, facing me, looking nervous.

"I'm Dr. Levine," I began. "What's your name?"

"Naisha," she answered, quietly.

"What brought you to the clinic today, Naisha?"

"The bus. Really, three buses."

"What time did you start? That's quite a long trip."

"First bus done left at 5, ma'am."

Polite and motivated, I liked her right away. I only hoped I would be able to help her. "Why did you come to the clinic?" I asked.

"All my friends is pregnant or have babies. I hardly never sees my monthly and I ain't never been pregnant." She paused, looking at her feet. "I guess I ain't right. Is it 'cause I'se fat?"

"Those are good questions," I said. "How often do you get your period?"

"About two or three times a year," she answered.

I told her that she probably was not ovulating, that her ovary was not releasing an egg every month.

Not releasing the egg may have been contributing to her obesity, because of the hormone imbalance of excess androgens. On the other hand, once you were obese, the extra fat could prevent you from ovulating because you convert fat into estrogen, which stops you from ovulating. I decided not to go into all of that at the moment, but focused on her concerns.

"Are you in a relationship? Are you having sex?" I asked. It's always so hard to find a way to say that. I can say "vagina," but I can't say "sexual intercourse."

"Yes ma'am," she answered politely.

"How long has that been?"

"Like, with my boyfriend, you mean, ma'am?" she asked earnestly, trying to please me.

"No, actually. I meant to ask, how many years have you been having sex? How old were you the first time?"

"Thirteen. That would be three years, right? And I ain't never gotten pregnant. That ain't right, is it?"

I sat down and looked into her dark, brown eyes. "Tell me," I said, 'Do you really want to have a baby right now?"

She looked back at me with big eyes, filled with such innocence, looking at me for help. Her shiny, brown skin framed a beautiful, if somewhat large, face, already plagued with some dark hairs along her cheeks and chin. "No," she began. "I'm just scared. I'm scared something's the matter with me. All my friends is pregnant, and I ain't."

Funny, I felt the same way. But, I was 30. All of my friends should be pregnant. And, so should I. When I was sixteen, I was worried about getting a date for the prom, and there was not going to be any sex after the prom. At sixteen, I would have worried about getting pregnant. It never crossed my mind to worry about not getting pregnant. But, I was, certainly, that day of all days, sympathetic to her plight.

"There are some tests that we can do," I assured her. "There are also medicines that you can take to make you ovulate, or release an egg, when you are ready. For now, though, I think that we should get you started on some birth control pills to get your periods regular. Do you smoke?"

"No," she said. She seemed like such a good kid. I wished that I could help her more, say something that would inspire her to go to college.

"What do you want to do when you finish high school?" I asked.

"Probably get me a job."

"Have you thought about college?" I asked.

She squinted her eyes as if the sun had glared through into our windowless exam room. "No, not really. I'll just get me a job."

"It might help you get a better job," I encouraged her, wondering where you start when you're starting with nothing at 16. She smiled, so I boldy continued, "Losing weight would help, too. It would help you get your period back. What do you do for exercise?"

"I works after school, ma'am," she replied.

"Do you have time to walk twenty minutes a day, either before or after school?" I asked.

"I can try," she offered.

"What do you usually eat for breakfast?" I asked, hoping to do some nutritional counseling.

"Ma'am, I don't eat no breakfast. I jist go to school, and I eats my meal at The Waffle House, after work. We git free waffles after our shift."

As I left the room while she undressed for an exam, I wondered if she could also get a free turkey sandwich or a salad. It did not sound as if there was any food at her house.

Her exam was normal except for size DD breasts, an overhanging belly called a pannus, her facial hair, and dark spots under her arms, consistent with an insulin resistance syndrome, not a body that could handle a diet of waffles and syrup.

I explained to her that she needed to have a pap smear every year to look for cancer.

"I heard the pill gives you cancer," she replied.

"No, the pill doesn't give you cancer. But sex can. Having sex with more than five men in your whole life, or having sex for the first time before you are 16 puts you at risk for cervical cancer. The pap smear looks for that type of cancer," I explained.

I excused myself and left the room to discuss the case with Dr. Taylor. Would Medicaid cover the cost of an HSG for a 16 year old? Should Medicaid cover the cost of an HSG for a 16 year old? We decided to start with some blood tests to check her hormones. The tests would check her thyroid function, rule out a brain tumor called a pituitary prolactinoma, evaluate her for something called polycystic ovarian syndrome, a condition in which your ovaries did not ovulate, and check a random blood sugar as a screen for diabetes. She should really come back for a fasting blood sugar and glucose challenge test, but she lived far away and it probably would not happen. He agreed with my plan to start birth control pills, but said it would be hard to get her a nutrition consult unless she ended up in the hospital for something or got pregnant. Since she hadn't eaten since the end of her shift the night before, her blood sugar might be normal by now.

I returned with two months worth of samples of birth control pills and gave her a prescription to fill after those were finished. I tried to explain the blood tests in as simple terms as I could, leaving out the term "brain tumor," and told her to come back in a week to discuss her results.

"I don't know if I can make it back here, ma'am."

"Can I call you?"

"We don't have no phone."

"Is there an address where I can send you the results?" I tried.

"We're by my auntie, now. You could send it there."

I took down the address and wished her luck, reminding her to try to walk every day and to think about college.

Most of the other patients that morning were missing their periods for one reason or another. Not me. Mine came every month, like clock work, blaring at me in big red stains and cramps that I was not pregnant. Your period is a bad time to find out that you are not pregnant. It's just not your best coping day of the month.

In the clinic, everyone who is late for their period gets a pregnancy test. One of my patients, a thin, white woman, with spaces between her crooked teeth, sunken cheeks, and flat sandy brown hair plastered to her head, had not had a period for six months. She was concerned that the combination of not getting her period, and her belly getting bigger might mean that she had cancer. A nurse popped her head in the room to tell me that the patient's pregnancy test was positive.

The woman looked at me quizzically.

"Please sit on the exam table for me," I requested. We had been sitting, facing each other, she in a vinyl patient chair and me on a wheely doctor stool.

Her weathered skin and teeth either missing or tobacco stained made her look like she was 50 years old, but her chart said that she was 32.

The obstetric clinic was held in the same rooms as the fertility clinic and the equipment was fortunately still in the drawer. I took out a tape measure. 28 centimeters. That was close enough. The baby was probably growth restricted from all of the cigarettes. I took out the Doppler and placed it on her belly. Good healthy heart tones. I even saw the baby kick. How could she not have felt it?

"Would you like a hand to sit up," I offered.

"No thanks." she said, looking totally unaffected by all of this.

"Well, you're definitely pregnant," I began, trying to read her distant blue eyes. "Is this good news?"

"So, it ain't cancer?"

"No, it's not. It's a baby," I paused. "Have you felt it moving?"

"It ain't cancer?"

"No, Joyce," I said, glancing at her chart to see her name. "You're pregnant."

I noticed that her chart was quite thick. I like to talk to patients first, get to know them a bit, before I look through their chart. It was time to look through the chart. Joyce was schizophrenic and mentally retarded, now called intellectually challenged, and lived in a presumably supervised, adult, assisted-living group home. She was on a long list of medications, including some which could cause birth defects.

"Do you have a boyfriend?" I asked.

"Yeah, me and Jake. He gets me cigarettes." She nodded and smiled.

"Excuse me a moment," I said. I picked up her heavy chart and found an empty office with a telephone on a steel, grayish blue desk. The desk felt nice and cold under my sweaty palms. Who was going to take care of this baby? What type of problems was it going to have? She was already thirty weeks into her pregnancy. She did not have long to come to terms with this and for the social worker to make arrangements.

I looked through the chart. She had been brought to the clinic every three months for her Depot Provera birth control shots until a year ago. I could not tell what had happened after that. It looked as if she had moved. I finally found the number of her psychiatrist and dialed that number. It belonged to someone else. The resident who had been her most recent psychiatrist had graduated. "Do you know about Joyce Smith?" I asked hopefully.

"Nope."

"Who is taking over Dr. Snell's patients?" I asked.

"They go to whomever is at the clinic when they first come. I can give you that number," the voice at the end of the phone answered.

There would certainly be a six week wait. "No, thanks," I said. "Are you a psychiatry resident?"

"Yes," the voice answered tentatively, suspecting that he was about to get a real doozy.

"Well, I need your help. This is Amy Levine, over in OB. I have a schizophrenic, mentally retarded patient who is suddenly 30 weeks pregnant. She needs to be seen today. She needs to have some time to deal with this before the baby comes."

"Why didn't you call sooner?"

"She just, we just, found out that she was pregnant. She thought she had cancer. Anyway, where should I send her? I can't just send her back to her group home. I think she needs to talk to someone."

"Let me call you back. What's your number?"

I gave the voice my pager number and paged the OB social worker.

"Boy, do I have a challenge for you," I told the social worker when she called me back. I told her the situation and said, "You'll need to come over to the clinic to see her. I don't think she would be able to follow directions to find you at the hospital."

I went back in to the exam room. Joyce was sitting right where I had left her, staring at the same spot. "Joyce," I said, "a nice lady is going to come and talk to you in a few minutes. Do you remember that I told you that you were pregnant?"

"Can I have a cigarette?" was her answer.

"Sorry, no smoking in the building. The nice lady will be here in a few minutes."

I put a note on her chart for the receptionist to make her an appointment for the High Risk Obstetric Clinic, and to have an ultrasound before the end of the week.

I saw a few more patients before the end of clinic and almost forgot to ask Dr. Taylor about the next step for me. We were heading down the stairs to the shuttle, discussing polycystic ovarian syndrome and its relationship to insulin resistance when I saw the social worker heading over to see Joyce. That reminded me of how unfair life was. Unfair for Joyce. I certainly would not trade places with her for the world. Unfair to me. Why could she get pregnant and not me?

Without wanting to seem too pushy, I guided our conversation to my own predicament. "So, what do you think about my HSG?" I asked.

As I suspected, Dr. Taylor suggested that I have a laparoscopy to look inside and then proceed from there.

Gathering up my nerve, I answered, "Can I try an MRI first, so I know what surgery I need. That way you won't be stuck in the OR with a long case when you thought it was just a quick look and see."

"Sure, an MRI is reasonable. They are just so expensive."

Expensive? Expensive compared to what? An unnecessary surgery? An unnecessary hole in my belly button? Actually, if I had intended to have Dr. Taylor do either a septum resection or the bicornuate repair it would not have mattered and it would have saved me a step. But, I happened to know that repairs of bicornuate uteruses are not done that often. I had not even decided if that's what I would do. I wanted to be awake and armed with information to make the decision myself, not asleep on the OR table and wake up to find that my uterus had been sliced to smithereens.

"Thanks, I'll go schedule it now," I said as the shuttle pulled up. As Dr. Taylor waved and walked outside to the shuttle, I turned around and went back to the clinic to spend the remaining 20 minutes that should have been for lunch working with the receptionist to schedule my MRI.

My mother called that night, to ask how I was doing, and if I was taking care of myself. Steven and I had just finished washing the dinner dishes, and I was already tucked in bed to try to get a good night's sleep, since I was on call again the next night.

"I'm fine," I answered.

"Did you have lunch today?" she asked.

How did she know? I wondered, as I answered, "No, but I had breakfast and dinner." I counted a granola bar and an apple in the car on the way to work as a full breakfast, but there was no reason to elaborate on this with my mother.

"Do you have a refrigerator where you can keep one of those protein drinks?" she persisted.

"Those taste awful," I replied.

"The chocolate ones aren't bad."

"Tomorrow, there is a lecture during lunch. I'll eat then." I pictured Mom, sitting in her office at home, in her big, black leather high back swivel chair, at her Danish wooden desk, full of papers. The slightly yellowed clock with gold numbers had been there for as long as I could remember. I used to lie on the couch behind her desk, watching her work, watching the gold second hand move slowly around the electric clock. The forest scene lamp that I had made at summer camp one year still cast light on her work.

"How is Steven? Is he enjoying his job?"

"Mom, I have to go to sleep." It was 7 p.m. "I'm on call tomorrow."

"Weren't you just on call last night?"

"Yes. Someone is on vacation and someone is sick."

"Can't they hire someone to fill in?"

"Mom," I said, exasperated, "you can not just hire a chief resident for a week or two."

"I thought there were laws about working those long hours."

"Only in New York, and only in internal medicine. They are wimps up there. Besides, I would be a resident forever if we only worked eight hours a day."

"Well, sweet dreams, sweet heart."

I had not mentioned my uterus. I did not want to hear her suggestions for improvement. I did not want her to know that I was weak, a failure, and defective, all at the same time and from the same thing. By asking me about my eating and sleeping, she seemed to know that my body suffered a fair amount of abuse and probably could not get pregnant, that no baby would want to grow in my body. I needed to go to sleep. Mom would want me to get my sleep. Tick tock, I heard the alarm clock next to me ticking away my precious moments of sleep. Tick tock, ticking away minutes, hours, days, weeks, months and years. I shouldn't be too old, yet. I couldn't be too old yet. I had delivered lots of women older than thirty. Should I stop? At some point, should I just stop the clock? Was my alarm going off? I had been working so hard for so long to get here. Did I have to give it all up to have a baby? Maybe my body just couldn't handle it all.

CHAPTER 4

▼

ANOTHER 38 HOUR DAY

The MRI was great, a welcome reprieve at the end of a 36 hour day, the kind that was now illegal in New York, but was what made us giants in North Carolina. I had been up the entire night before; my head had not touched the pillow. In fact, I had been so busy that I had not even seen the sleep room. As it turned out, the lunch that I had promised my mother was probably not what she would have chosen. The lecture topic was risk factors for breast cancer. One risk factor was the correlation between fat in the diet and breast cancer. Since lunch was cold pizza, with the cheese already congealed into glassy fat globules by the time I arrived, I had to wonder if it was better to eat the pizza and stimulate breast cancer cells or to skip lunch with whatever dire consequences my mother thought that might have. The other risk factor for breast cancer, further killing my appetite for cold, congealed pizza, was delayed child-bearing, "delayed" being after 30 years old. I chewed on some crust before heading out to see my afternoon patients.

After I finished my afternoon clinic, I tracked down Dr. Stanis, a small woman with compassionate brown eyes, a soft voice, and light brown hair always hanging freely to her shoulders, and the least frightening of all the attendings, despite her hundreds of publications. As nonchalantly as I could, I asked her to write me a prescription for ten milligrams of Valium. Since I only asked for one, and since I was hardly the drug abusing type, I hoped that she would not ask too many questions. Everyone knew that I had too much of a Type A personality to develop a Valium problem. In my trim forest green dress under my white coat, single strand of pearls and hair neatly held in a headband, I looked quite responsible, not the "druggy" type. Saying as little as I could, I explained that I was having an MRI and asked if she could write the prescription for me. As I expected, she was very kind and wished me luck, probably guessing exactly what was going on. She did not ask why I was having an MRI and I did not volunteer. I thought that my attendings, even the women, would hate it if I got pregnant, because that meant maternity leave and making everyone else work harder.

I had heard that some people had to stop their MRI in the middle due to claustrophobia, caused by the closed capsule and disturbing banging noises, like drill hammers against your head.

As I sat in the waiting room in the radiology department, I noticed that I was at least 30 years younger than any of the other patients. Maybe this was an extravagant test. I rested my sleep deprived head in my hands.

"Amy Levine! Excuse me, are you Miss Levine?" The nice receptionist called as she touched my head.

"Oh, yes, sorry," I said, forcing open my heavy eyelids as quickly as I could.

"You can go back now."

I followed a handsome, young, black man in scrubs, who directed me to a dressing room. Fortunately, there was a water fountain in the dressing room and I surreptitiously swallowed my Valium. Maybe I should have started with 5 mg. Maybe it was dangerous to take when I was already so tired. How long would this take to work? What it if did not work in time? Mom would definitely not have wanted me to start out with ten milligrams, but what was the danger? To me, the biggest danger would be having to reschedule the MRI, which would mean possibly canceling patients or asking someone to cover for me, and delaying the diagnosis of my freak uterus. Maybe, I should have taken twenty milligrams.

The young man was waiting when I came out, decked out in my lovely hospital gown, with its signature opening in the back. Was that really necessary, to have your butt hanging out in the hallway in order to get an adequate picture on an MRI? Anyway, I thought I had one of the better looking butts in that particular hallway.

I followed the technician into a cavernous white room. Although I had walked past that room many times, now that I was inside, it looked much more imposing. I imagined the sound of drill hammers next to my ears as I lay in the cold machine.

On the brighter side, that long, thin slab of table coming phallicly out of the circular machine offered a place to hide my exposed bottom and to lie down. My eyelids drooping from having been up all night, I eagerly followed the technician's directions to lie down.

Lying down, with my eyes closed, I tried to concentrate. There was some whirring and some movement. Within moments, I was sound asleep. "Breathe, don't forget to breathe," a voice said, several times. How rude to wake me up like that.

All too soon, they told me it was time to get up. I was so comfortable, and asleep. I managed to pull myself up and followed the directions back to the dressing room.

After changing my patient clothing for doctor clothing, I went in search of a radiologist to read my MRI for me.

There was a corridor of rooms of radiologists, residents and attendings, reading X-Rays and CT scans. They were all in large groups, and I did not want to interrupt anyone or call attention to myself. Finally, I found an attending alone in a room with X-rays.

"Excuse me," I said, timidly. "I just had an MRI and I was hoping you could look at it for me."

"*You* had one?" the radiologist asked, with genuine concern. He had a dark complexion, a slight accent and black hair, graying slightly around the temples. His wire rimmed glasses gave him a professorial look.

"Oh, it's just for infertility," I answered, at once relieved and somewhat embarrassed that I was bothering him for something that was certainly not an emergency. It was not a life or death situation, just life or not life for my future family.

"What room were you in?" he asked, still kindly.

"Oh, I don't know," I answered, wondering if now I would have to wait until the MRI's were read the following afternoon.

"We'll find it," he said. "Follow me. Did you have an MRI of the abdomen and pelvis or just pelvis?"

Thank God for the Valium. I would have died if one of my OB/GYN attendings asked me two questions in a row that I had to answer, "I don't know." How could you not know such basic things, what room number you were in and what body parts were pictured in your own MRI? Usually, you only need a patient's birthday to pull up results on the computer. This time, the one time I knew the patient's birthday, it did not matter. "They were checking to see if the uterus was bicornuate or had a septum." I could not bring myself to say *my* uterus." I refrained from adding that the HSG looked really awful. I barely managed to hold back tears; I still had not had a chance to cry over all of this yet.

"Probably just the pelvis, then," he said in his kind accent. "Unless, they were worried about your kidneys." As I followed him down the hall, I noticed the name on his white coat. He was the chairman of the entire radiology department. Surely, he did not have time for this type of piddly problem.

I had forgotten that uterine abnormalities often go along with kidney abnormalities. How much of me could be defective?

I followed his starched white coat, gray slacks and well-polished black shoes along a maze of stark white corridors. He stuck his head into several rooms and asked if anyone had just done an MRI of the pelvis.

Eventually, we found the right room and the technician pulled the images up on the computer screen. He hit some buttons and complex black, grey and white images flashed quickly past, like the old-fashioned movie box in Disney World.

"Stop there," the radiologist said.

"Look at this," he pointed out. "You're an OB/GYN resident," he said, reading the name and title on my white coat. "Maybe you'll recognize this."

"Oh, please, don't make me guess," I prayed, silently.

"This is the uterus," the radiologist continued.

I held my breath. It looked like a smooth contour, but I could never tell how the MRI machine "sliced" things.

"Is that a smooth contour?" I ventured, no longer worried about exposing any lack of knowledge, but hoping against hope that this time I had the lesser of two evils in my impressively infertile body.

"Yes," he answered. "The uterine contour is intact. Here are the fallopian tubes and the ovaries. This must be a septum."

"Thank you," I sighed, barely suppressing an urge to hug him. "Thank you, so much." Finally, some good news.

I was beyond exhaustion, emotionally and physically. My head was spinning. I thought it might be the Valium. After leaving the room, I found a phone and called my husband to come pick me up. I did not think that I could force myself to focus on the road to drive home, no matter how raucous the country western music might have been that afternoon.

I sat in front of the hospital, staring into a lovely, Valium haze. Steven pulled up in his second hand, dusty, brown Honda Civic. He reached across and swung open the door for me. The air conditioner rattled as it valiantly fought against the North Carolina heat. He was wearing flip flops, his running shorts, a Yale t-shirt and a smile, much better clothing for a car with weak air conditioning at best, than my cotton dress with rayon-lining, pantyhose and a white coat. And, I was certainly not wearing a smile, although I was glad to see Steven. I did not have enough energy to elevate the corners of my lips.

I plopped into the seat, the stethoscope around my neck bouncing and banging into my chest.

"You can take your white coat off, now," Steven laughed. "Otherwise, you might melt in here. If it stays this hot, I might finally have to replace the air conditioning in this car."

As I shimmied out of my white coat, working up more of a sweat than if I had kept it on, Steven asked, "Are you okay?"

"What a day," I said, leaning my head against the stained headrest and closing my eyes. "Good news, though. I only have a septum. I'm so relieved."

"How was the MRI? I read that they can be quite frightening," he said, his voice full of concern.

"Nothing a little sleep deprivation and ten milligrams of Valium couldn't handle," I laughed. "Great place to sleep. Good firm support for the back, but they kept yelling at me to breath, waking me up."

We both laughed.

He reached over the stick shift and squeezed my hand. "Don't be all nice to me. You'll make me cry," I said, squeezing my eyes shut.

The phone rang while we were eating dinner. Steven picked up the receiver and handed it to me, knowing who it was without even asking. Sure enough, it was Mom, exactly thirty minutes earlier than she had called the other night, when I had already been in bed. I had a sneaking suspicion that she knew that something was up. I almost told her that I was loopy from Valium, just to hear her fret, but I realized, just in time, that I would then have to explain why I had taken Valium.

"I had lunch, Mom," I said, choosing a different route of evasion.

"Good. What was it?"

"Breast cancer pizza."

"What kind of pizza?" she asked.

"They had a lecture on how fat causes breast cancer and fed us pizza. It would not have been my first choice for the menu, given the topic. It was cold by the time I got there, anyway."

"Did they have a salad?"

"A salad?" I repeated.

"Some places that deliver pizza will deliver salad," Mom explained.

"That would require plates and forks, and more money," I retorted.

"I wish I could be there to take care of you."

"Steven and I are having salad with dinner. Right now, in fact."

"Oh, am I interrupting dinner? Well, when is a good time to call?" Mom asked.

"Never," I answered. "I'm hardly ever home and awake. Maybe on the weekend. Do you remember my friend Stacey?"

"Didn't she have breast cancer?" Mom answered.

"Yes," I replied. "She died last week. She had a baby, you know. Not even a year old. She made a video tape of herself reading and singing so her baby will remember her."

"I don't remember you telling me that she was pregnant. Did she get pregnant after she had breast cancer?"

I knew that Mom, sitting at her yellow, 70's era eat-in kitchenette covered with work papers, was thinking that Stacey had hastened her death by getting pregnant. Stacy and I had had long talks before she got pregnant. It had not been an easy decision, but she had decided that she was going to live her life as she wanted, and she wanted a child. I told my mother what Stacey and I had discussed, and what I'm sure Stacey and her husband had discussed. "Her mother died at 39 of breast cancer. I don't think it would have made any difference if she didn't have the baby. Now, at least, her husband has their baby."

From the tone of Mom's question, I thought that she would have chosen Stacey over the baby. Maybe she would still love me when I told her that I couldn't have children. But, I wasn't going to have that conversation tonight.

CHAPTER 5

▼

THE SURGERY SCHEDULE

The next morning, I found Dr. Taylor and told him the good news about my MRI. "Guess what," I said breathlessly, certain that he would be as excited as I was. "It's just a septum! When can we do a hysteroscopy? I'm already scheduled to be out in April. Can we do it that week?"

"Let's sit in my office for a minute," Dr. Taylor said, leading me down the fluorescent white hall.

I glanced at my watch. Tick tock. I was due to be in clinic in five minutes. Well, that would just have to wait. I had put this on hold for seven years; clinic could wait a few minutes.

We sat in Dr. Taylor's office. There were no windows in this basement infertility department. It all looked white and sterile. In this office, he had more pictures of his wife and children on his desk. There was a Persian, or an imitation Persian, rug on the floor. On the wall was a framed print of a brook running through the woods, the sun shining on the quickly flowing water. But, the office still looked stark. The book shelves were full of thick textbooks, some of which I had at home.

Dr. Taylor began, "Septums are usually associated with recurrent miscarriages, not with infertility. Surgery may not be necessary. As you know, surgery always has risks."

That had not occurred to me. I have a problem; we should fix it. I have always been a "doer," a "problem fixer," not a "wait and see" person. I thought quickly,

"Well, if I do finally get pregnant, I don't want to have a miscarriage. I'd like to get rid of the septum." What did I know? He was the fancy university attending, but it just did not seem right to wait for a miscarriage, and certainly not for two miscarriages.

"Just think about it," he answered, calmly.

I nodded, feeling defeated. I really did not want to go through all of this just to have a miscarriage. I saw miscarriages almost every call night in the emergency room. Sometimes women were bleeding so heavily that they had to be rushed to the operating room to have the remaining pregnancy tissue removed by a procedure called dilation and curettage. Sometimes they came innocently to the clinic, never suspecting that the baby had died. It always seemed devastating to me.

Later that afternoon, I tracked down Dr. Taylor. "I'd like to have the surgery," I said, with a surgeon's confidence.

He said that he would check with his secretary. He operated on Thursdays. A Thursday surgery should give me plenty of time to recover and be back to work at 5:30 Monday morning. I knew that a hysteroscopy was an outpatient procedure with no incisions and should not require a prolonged recovery. Nonetheless, I would have preferred to do it earlier during my vacation week, just in case I needed a few extra days. But, surgery days were surgery days. I could not expect the world to change, clinic patients to be rescheduled, for my sake.

Later that day, I called my mother. Her wish had come true, she would be able to come down and take care of me, at least for a few days. The only other surgery that I had ever had was to have my wisdom teeth removed. The surgery had been done under general anesthesia, in a hospital, and I vividly remembered my mother being there when I woke up. Her presence had been very comforting. I knew that she would want to be there. And, I wanted her there. Even though the hysteroscopy was "just outpatient surgery," it still made me want my mommy.

I had not yet told her about the septum.

When I called her that night, her first response was, "What causes a uterine septum? Does it grow with age?"

"This is not my fault, mother," I snapped defensively. "I was born with this."

"It's a birth defect," clanged through my mind. "Now, you have a defective child," I thought. I had always done well in school, dated nice boys, gone to medical school, and now, I was defective, a failure.

Talking to my mother, I finally started to cry. This was the person I had disappointed the most—my mother. I wanted to give her everything. I had done everything right, and now I had screwed up! I could not do the most basic human, or even animal, task; I could not have a baby!

I just sobbed into the phone. It sounded to me as if she were trying not to cry on the other end; her breaths sounded a bit heavy and long. Steven put his comforting, strong hands on my shoulders, then slipped them around my waist.

"Tell me about the septum," she said, when I had stopped crying enough to hear anything.

"Well, they can usually be fixed," I started, trying to collect myself and sound cheerful. "At first, we thought that it might be something worse."

"What's worse?" she asked. How could she ask that? Did she think that I had the worst defect in the entire world? What's worse?

"A bicornuate uterus, a uterus with two horns. That's worse," I answered, again defensively, as though she were accusing me of having the worst possible thing, as if I had not set her up to ask that.

"How do you fix it?" she asked.

I explained what a hysteroscopy was, that it was an outpatient procedure and that I would not have to miss any work, that we were going to do it at the end of my vacation week. "Some vacation," I joked.

"Can't you take off any more time? Thursday to Sunday is not a long time to recover."

"No, Mom," I retorted. "That's plenty of time. I could probably go back the next day." Why did she always have such unrealistic requests? I was an OB resident; you did not just go taking time off.

Despite my snapping at her several times while she was trying to be helpful and to digest the bits and pieces of information that I threw at her as if she spoke my OB/GYN language, she promised to be here for my surgery and through the weekend.

The next day, Dr. Taylor found me. He had looked at the MRI and talked to Dr. Marks, the head of the infertility department. They thought that it would be a good idea to do a laparoscopy at the time of the hysteroscopy. The septum was pretty thick, and by looking from above, they could be careful not to puncture the uterus. And, they could look for endometriosis.

Great. Endometriosis, another condition that can cause infertility. Did I want to know that in addition to not ovulating and having a defective uterus I might also have endometriosis? Not really. At least, that wasn't my fault, either. Endometriosis is a condition of uterine lining cells outside the uterus, usually in your pelvis. No one is quite sure how the cells get there or why they interfere with getting pregnant, but there are lots of theories. My favorite theory is that the cells come out of your tubes into the pelvis with your period, and that they cause an inflammatory reaction that interferes with pregnancy. The other popular theory involves embryology; the cells that line the pelvis are similar to those that line the uterus and the uterine lining cells just grow in the wrong place.

A laparoscopy and a laparoscopy with a hysteroscopy are both outpatient procedures. The laparoscopy involves making several incisions, the largest in the belly button and other, smaller, incisions, usually along the bikini line. Usually, the belly button incision is used for the camera and the smaller ones are used to insert instruments into the pelvis to perform the surgery, like a video game.

"Do you still think I can be back to work on Monday, if we do it on Thursday?" I asked, feeling that I should know this, since I counseled patients for, and, in fact, did this surgery all the time. Mostly, I was hoping that he might volunteer to do it earlier in the week.

"I think so," he said. "I'll have my secretary set it up."

At the end of clinic the day before my husband and I left for our much abbreviated vacation, I stopped at the admissions area of the hospital. After writing out in my own history and physical, I filled in the details and signed my consent form. I ordered my blood work and went to the lab to have it drawn. If I could have, I would have drawn my own blood, but I could not quite figure out how to manipulate the needles and the tubes with one hand.

The vacation was a blur; I could not even tell you where we went. Wherever we went, walking on a beach, strolling through the woods, I tried to be cheerful and calm, but I could not help thinking about the one in ten-thousand people who never wake up from anesthesia. The electric cutting loop that would be used to remove my septum might go all the way through the wall of my uterus and burn a chunk of my intestines. If that happened, I might end up with not only a hysterectomy, but also with a colostomy bag. Instead of carrying a baby in my arms, I would be wearing stool in a plastic bag on my stomach. Maybe, I should have waited for the surgery. Maybe, I was just not meant to have children.

"Are you all right?" Steven asked, when I embarked on one of these silent self-torture sessions.

"What do you mean?" I answered. I wasn't about to share these ridiculous fears with him. Feeling like enough of a failure, I didn't want to be an idiot on top of that.

"You're quiet," he answered, "in a different sort of way."

"Oh, I'm just tired from making up all the extra calls for vacation," I fibbed.

When we came back the night before the surgery, I had to go to the hospital to have a laminaria put into my cervix. Laminaria are thin cylinders of seaweed that have the amazing property of causing the cervix, which is the opening of the uterus at the end of the vagina, to open. How on earth did someone figure out that if you rammed seaweed inside your vagina that it made your uterus contract?

Steven drove me right to the hospital and I paged my friend, Janis, who was the chief resident on call that night. She met us in the exam room on the GYN floor. The room had an empty off-white desk with a telephone, blue cupboards above a shelf with a sink, a very new, blue gynecologic chair, (the kind where you raise the back of the feet with foot pedals), a doctor's stool on wheels and an adjustable floor light.

I found a sheet in one of the cupboards, pulled down some new paper onto the exam table, scooted off my bottoms, covered myself with the sheet and hopped onto the table. Steven and Janis were chatting outside the door.

"I'm ready," I called.

Janis, a tall, blond woman with a perfect complexion, short, wavy hair, a trace of a southern accent, and an easy smile, had everything that she needed in the pocket of her white coat. Speculums were kept in a drawer in the exam chair.

Steven stood next to me and held my hand. That was a good place for him to be. Supportive as he was, he was not a blood and guts kind of guy. Although he liked to tinker with things around the house, enjoyed any opportunity to use his electric drill, and I always called him to change my flat tires, he did not particularly relish the detailed discussions of medical disasters at resident dinners. Holding my hand and facing me during the little procedure, he would not have to see anything "down there." Not that he had not seen it, but the metal bladed speculum and the view into the deep, dark vagina might take away what little romance and mystery were left in the bedroom once the quest for fertility changed from passion to science.

She was quite gentle with the speculum. She cleaned off the cervix with betadyne and then tried to put in the laminaria. Of course, my cervix was too tight to allow even this small cylinder to pass. I clenched Steven's hand as she grasped my cervix with a single-tooth tenaculum, a pointy, sharp grasping instrument, and then used small metal rods to dilate, or open, my cervix until it was open enough to push in the laminaria. "Sorry," she said.

"Oh, don't worry about it. Thanks so much for doing this tonight," I answered through gritted teeth.

"Boy, am I glad I'm not a woman," Steven joked. "Those are some viscious-looking instruments. Did you steal them from a medieval torture exhibit?"

"I use those all the time. All day, every day," I laughed.

Once Janis had removed all the metal instruments from inside of me, I felt better, but the laminaria, which was to stay in all night, still caused some painful pressure.

"Good luck tomorrow," she said, as she headed out, so that I could dress in private.

"Those really look like medieval torture instruments," Steven could not help saying again. "I wish they didn't have to do that to you."

"I use them every day," I answered. "You just get used to them. And, it really wasn't so bad. Still, I'd rather be the doctor than the patient."

When we got home, I was cramping slightly. Sitting on the bed, I called the operating room, just to make sure everything was still as planned. Much to my surprise, since no one had said anything to me or left me any messages, my surgery had been moved to Friday. Because I had a latex allergy, they couldn't operate on me in the outpatient surgery center. Not only had the surgery been moved to the main operating room, it had been moved to the next day.

There I sat, on my bed, cramping from the laminaria, feeling confused and abandoned. Dr. Taylor knew that Janis was putting in a laminaria the night before my surgery; we had arranged it, together, the three of us. You do not just leave in a laminaria for an extra day. It can cause an infection, an infection which can potentially, although rarely, cause infertility. Not what I needed right now. I was having trouble thinking clearly over the cramping, but could think enough to be overcome by disappointment. I wanted my mommy. She was coming in the next day, to take care of me while I recovered from my surgery. She had already given me a hard time for not taking enough time off from work to recover after my surgery. Now I would have one less day to recover.

I dialed her number.

"Hello," she answered, many miles away.

"You don't need to come tomorrow," I said. "My surgery has been moved to Friday."

"I already have my tickets. I can come spend the day with you."

That was logical; the possibility of just hanging around the house had not occurred to me. I was focused on the cramping from the laminaria, which I was not looking forward to enjoying for an extra day.

Mom, using that sixth sense that mother's have, asked, "Why was your surgery moved?"

"I have a latex allergy."

"Didn't you tell them at your pre-op visit?"

Why was everything my fault with her? "Yes," I answered, defensively, "I told them. I mentioned it several times and even had the nurse check with the anesthesiologist to make sure that there wouldn't be any problems."

"Can you take an extra day or two for your recovery?" she asked.

Although I was already worried about that, I didn't want to hear it from her. "No, I can't. I'm on the obstetric service. I've already been out for a week." She just didn't understand. I couldn't just "dump" on the other residents like that. You didn't just take an extra day, just like that, out of the blue, for no reason.

I couldn't tell her that, not only was I working on Monday, I was on call. To add to the challenge, I was chief on the busy obstetric service and it would be hard to avoid moving obese patients who were not only nine months pregnant, but swollen from fluid retention. They always seemed to need an emergency C-Section, and the residents, to expedite the process, help moved them onto the operating table.

"When did you find out?" she asked.

"I called you first. No one even told me. Janis already put in the laminaria. I had to call the operating room to find out." My voice was rising and my already rapid speech patterns were getting faster.

"What's a laminaria?"

I was totally annoyed at the question; the laminaria was not the point. She didn't know anything about my world. These people were supposed to be taking care of me. I was their resident and their patient. Now, they had moved my surgery, without telling me.

I snapped back, "It's seaweed that you use to dilate the cervix."

"Seaweed?"

"Yes, like sushi. Like you find in the ocean. I don't know who discovered that sticking seaweed into your cervix makes you contract, but we do it every day."

"Is it sterile?" she asked.

"I don't know. I guess so. It comes in a sealed container, and I wear sterile gloves when I put it in. Enough about the seaweed."

"Maybe the person you talked to made a mistake. I can't believe no one would have even left you a message."

Not true? "It seems like an odd mistake for the night clerk to make, but maybe. I guess I should just show up tomorrow and see."

"Why don't you call your doctor?"

"At home? At night?" I asked. What a ridiculous idea.

"I think it's reasonable, given the circumstances," she persisted. "It's not that late, and it *is* tomorrow. Maybe he can do something. I do think you need more time to recover. You hardly have any time as it is."

I did not want to hear about the recovery time, again. Why did she have to harp on that? I hadn't told her that a laparoscopy had been added to the hysteroscopy. I didn't want to bother Dr. Taylor at home. I wished that I could ask Mom to call him.

A big cramp caused me to gasp.

"What is it?" Mom asked.

"Nothing," I lied. "I better call Dr. Taylor now, if I'm going to call."

I called the operating room to get Dr. Taylor's home phone number. I hoped that he would not be home, and I could just leave a message on his machine. No such luck. His wife answered the phone.

"This is Amy Levine. I'm a resident, calling for Dr. Taylor," I explained.

"He's not on call tonight," she answered.

"I know," I replied. "I'm calling about my surgery for tomorrow."

"Oh," she replied, now sounding quite friendly, "I'll get him."

I wondered if she knew that it was *my* surgery, as in surgery on me, as opposed to *my* surgery that I was doing on someone else. Had he told her about the annoying resident who pestered him in the hallway about her infertility and then had a uterus from the bizarre uterus text book?

Dr. Taylor confirmed that it was true, that my surgery had, in fact, been moved. I refrained from asking if anyone was going to tell me about this change before I showed up tomorrow at 5 a.m. Should I keep the laminaria in until the surgery? I presumed that I should know the answer, that I should not leave it in past tomorrow morning. Or should I? Would my cervix close back up and my night of cramping be wasted? I didn't mention that I could have stayed on my much needed vacation a day longer. Instead, I surprised myself by asking, "Can you still do it tomorrow if I can get OR time?"

"That's an oncology surgery day, isn't it?" he asked, in return.

"Yes. I've been chief on that service. I might be able to do something."

"If you can get time, I can be there. Just let me know," he said. His voice sounded kind, but it didn't seem fair that I even had to reschedule my own surgery.

One of the more odious jobs of the chief resident was juggling the OR schedule and all of the egos involved therein. Now, I knew why I had that experience. Now, I knew how to try to save my extra day of recovery time.

I collected myself and called the OR for the third time that night. They told me that because of my latex allergy, my case would have to be first thing in the morning; if my case were moved, it would disrupt the entire day. *I* would disrupt the entire day.

It was looking like my surgery would remain on Friday with a two day recovery. "Who has the first case in the GYN room?" I asked. I could not move cases from the general surgery service. I could only do something within my own department. Thursday was the big operating day for the gynecologic oncology service and I prayed that the first case belonged to the one oncology attending who did not intimidate the hell out of me.

"Dr. Henner," the voice at the end of the line said.

That was worse than having a septum in the first place. He wasn't just a big wig locally; he was president of national and international organizations. Always dressed in a dapper suit when not in the operating room and with smooth skin that reflected a life of comfort, he was also director of the residency program and could make or break you. Of course, he had never been anything less than perfectly nice to me. We joked, talked about basketball and horses. He always had an easy smile for me, but he still scared me to death.

I called one of the oncology fellows at home. Fellows were beyond residency, doing additional specialized training. Stan was a very nice guy, and very low in the hierarchy, in training directly under Dr. Henner. I explained my problem; I was supposed to have surgery the next day, but it had been moved because of my latex allergy. I did not want to sound like a wimp, but I thought that losing a day of recovery time might be a problem, since I was on call on Monday. I decided not to mention that I was already miserable from the laminaria. He did not need to have an image in his mind of the brown, rolled up seaweed in my cervix.

Unfortunately, he said, he could not make that decision. He thought that the patient scheduled for first thing the next morning was some special family friend of Dr. Henner. I would have to talk directly to Dr. Henner.

I really didn't want to do that.

After hanging up with Stan, I called Steven into the room. "Will you hold my hand while I do this?" I asked.

My whole body was shaking as I dialed. I can't remember exactly what I said, but I explained that my surgery had been moved because of my latex allergy and that I had to be back to work on Monday and that the surgery would not take very long, so would it be ok if we just slipped it in first thing in the morning.

When I paused for a breath, Dr. Henner asked, "Are you the one having the surgery?" Residents always referred to any surgery they were doing as "my" surgery, so saying "my surgery," did not at all imply that I was having surgery.

"Yes, sir," I answered.

"Well, absolutely, I can start a little later. I'll enjoy an extra cup of coffee with my wife before coming in. Good luck." He didn't mention anything about the patient being a family friend.

"Thank you. I'll let the OR know."

"Have a good night. Bye, now."

I couldn't believe it. That was so easy. What had I been afraid of, anyway?

I called Dr. Taylor to let him know. He said he would call Dr. Marks and tell him. I called my new friend at the OR desk to let him know the change in the morning schedule, and to make sure that they would have the correct equipment ready. I didn't want Dr. Henner's case to be delayed any further.

When my heart slowed back to near its usual pace and stopped pounding in my ears, I laid down to try to sleep. Cramps kept me up all night, but that was nothing compared with conquering my nerves to call Dr. Henner.

The next morning, holding hands, Steven and I walked into the surgery waiting area about 5 a.m. It was in full swing, bright eyed people in blue scrub suits leading around somewhat anxious individuals in open-backed hospital gowns. I changed into my hospital gown, no longer worried about my butt sticking out, but making sure that there was material between my bottom and the cold plastic chair. A nurse's aide came to take my vitals.

Then, someone called me to come to a back room with two rows of stretchers vaguely hidden behind curtains. Steven and I followed the nurse. She looked skeptically at my chart. "We don't have a history and physical or a consent form," she said.

"My case got moved to this morning from Friday," I explained.

"They may be locked up with the charts for Friday's cases," the nurse said, thoughtfully. With brunette hair pulled into a neat pony tail just past her shoulders, diamond stud earrings, and an even tan along her face and through the V neck of the blue hospital scrubs, she was matter-of-fact, but did not seem to be phased by a potential delay. "We can't do anything until those are completed. I'll have to page your doctor."

"I can fill them in," I said quickly. "I'm an OB/GYN resident. I do these all the time." I wasn't about to have my surgery changed again. With my latex allergy, delaying the case would have meant canceling for the entire day. I also didn't want her to page Dr. Taylor at 5:30 a.m.

The nurse brought me the forms and I quickly filled them out, writing out the long list of risks of the procedures that I always reviewed with patients. I tilted the form away from Steven. I didn't want him to panic over the lines about quadriplegia, paraplegia, brain damage, cardiac arrest and death.

Next, the anesthesiologist came in, in the green scrubs reserved for doctors, and looked at my paperwork. "Your blood pressure is 62/40. Do you feel okay?"

"Yes, I'm fine," I assured him. "I'm a runner."

Some people are nervous when they are wheeled off to the OR. Not me; I was just relieved.

Nightmare patient that I was, I wanted an epidural, so that I could keep tabs on what was going on. I have a very clear recollection of Dr. Taylor and Dr. Marks walking into the room, talking to me, telling me that Dr. Marks would do the laparoscopy and Dr. Taylor would do the hysteroscopy.

I sat with my feet over the side of the bed for the epidural. While the anesthesiologist pressed my vertebrae, it finally made sense that the back of my hospital gown was open. I bent forward, "like a Cheshire cat" while he cleaned my spine with betadyne, then stuck in a needle. Youch! That really hurt, but I just grimaced silently.

After the epidural, I lay on the bed, and the doctors positioned me with my legs in the usual GYN position. I remember thinking that this would have been embarrassing if I could have felt my legs, but since they were numb, it was okay.

Dr. Marks made an incision in my belly button and inflated it with gas. Well, that hurt. Since I could not see the video screen, anyway, I asked the anesthesiologist to put me to sleep.

The next thing I knew, I was sitting in a chair in the recovery room. Steven and my mother were sitting next to me and a nurse was handing me a Sprite. I took a few sips of the Sprite and soon got to experience first hand what the term "projectile vomiting" really meant. How elegant.

What seemed like a few minutes later, Dr. Taylor strode into my curtained cubicle in the recovery room. He told me that taking out the septum had taken longer than expected and that I had bled quite a bit.

"How long?" I asked, "because I promised Dr. Henner that it wouldn't be a long case."

"Don't worry about that," Dr. Taylor reassured me, with a laugh. "I think they got him started in another room."

Wow, I had screwed up the whole OR schedule.

Dr. Taylor showed me the pictures, as I had shown my patients so many times. "This is your uterus, and these are your fallopian tubes and ovaries. Here, on your ovary, and in the cul de sac (the space behind your uterus if you lift it up) is some endometriosis. I'd call it Stage II. You know, your best chance of getting pregnant is in the first six months after a laparoscopy."

I nodded in my still drugged haze. "Thanks."

"Maybe the endometriosis was the problem all along," he said, reassuringly.

"I'm Dr. Levine," my mother said, standing up to introduce herself. (Where were my manners?) "Do you really think she can go back to work on Monday?"

I was too tired from anesthesia, and from just having thrown up, and from having just been told that I had yet another cause of infertility, to be angry with her. Just embarrassed. "Oh, Mom," I said. How could she be trying to make me miss more work at a time like this?

"I think she will be fine," Dr. Taylor said. "I'm sure she'll be in excellent hands. Nice to meet you," he said, before turning to leave.

"Well?" I asked my mother expectantly, thinking that she would be very impressed at what a pleasant, good-looking doctor I had.

"He's so tall. And such a surgeon's attitude," she responded.

How could she have said that? He was one of the mildest mannered guys around here. And, I couldn't help it if he was tall.

The nurse came by a few minutes later. I had not thrown up since the Sprite and she told me that I could go home.

My mother asked her to please review my restrictions, so that I would not try to go jogging that afternoon. Between Steven and my mother, there would be no escape, even if I felt better.

I was an obedient patient all weekend. I ate jell-o and chicken broth. Friday passed quickly. On Saturday, I convinced my caregivers/captors to let me go for a walk. My belly was a bit sore, and the incisions occasionally caused a small stabbing pain. I shuffled through our small apartment, down the wooden stairs and around the flat parking lot. It was a glorious summer morning. The sun was out, the birds were singing and a light breeze was blowing. One day, maybe I would be taking a child out in a stroller on a day like this.

CHAPTER 6

▼

THE FASTEST RECOVERY

Monday morning, I sprang out of bed at 4:45 a.m. and was in the hospital reviewing charts of the 30 patients on my obstetric service by 5:30 a.m. By 7:45 a.m., in time to present to the team of attending physicians, I had met all of the complicated patients who would be my primary responsibility for the day.

Shauna, a picture of strength at 5 feet, eight inches tall, with hands that had worked in the tobacco fields for years and, except for her stained hands, beautiful, shiny black skin, had an "incompetent cervix." Without any warning, she had suddenly lost babies at 20 and 24 weeks. Her cervix had silently dilated, just opened up, without contractions. We were keeping her in the hospital on bed rest. Despite warnings after her previous pregnancies, she had not come in for prenatal care until 22 weeks. We might have been able to put a stitch in her cervix to keep it closed had she come in earlier. A rescue cerclage or stitch to hold the cervix closed was still not out of the question, but much riskier than it would have been at 12 or 14 weeks.

A uterine septum increased the risk of cervical incompetence. I wondered if I ever got pregnant, if I would have an incompetent cervix. Probably. I had every thing else that was bad. Would I have to miscarry to find out, or should I just have a stitch put in early? Of course, putting in a stitch could cause your water to break and cause you, meaning me, to lose the pregnancy.

My next two patients were two teenage cocaine addicts, Anna and Tiffany, kept at opposite ends of the hall, were basically under unofficial hospital arrest to keep them off the street. They took the shuttle from the hospital to the clinic twice a week, on different days, for drug rehabilitation therapy, and often returned with positive drug screens. Tiffany was pregnant with twins and also had an incompetent cervix. When she was only 24 weeks pregnant and her cervix already 4 centimeters dilated (it was supposed to be closed, or not dilated at all), she had gotten off the shuttle and walked the quarter mile to the clinic so that she could smoke a joint. That was before I had gone on vacation. I brought it up with her this morning, emphasizing that 26 week babies were still not ready to be born. She seemed to respect my candidness and concern.

Maribelle was a nurse in the neurosurgery intensive care unit whose unborn baby was not growing well and had low fluid. Maribelle had been to nursing school in Sweden, before marrying a U.S serviceman and moving to the United States. Her husband and her family were far away, but, she had made a lot friends and had a flow of visitors from the ICU at each shift change. She had pictures of her family, all tall and blond like her, pinned to her bulletin board. Her husband, not quite as tall as her father and brothers, was the brunette. They seemed to be smiling right at her. Her sparkling blue eyes remained optimistic, and we all hoped that her indefatigable spirit would flow through her placenta to the baby. The baby was monitored daily by ultrasound to make sure that there was still blood flow through the placenta to the baby. She was on bed rest and getting fluids through an I.V. to help get fluid to the baby. She also went to hydrotherapy in a whirlpool every day. She was doing everything she could for her baby.

Another patient, an Ethiopian woman so thin that even her light black skin seemed thin, had a baby with a cardiac arrhythmia, an irregular heartbeat. In an effort to convert the baby's heart rate to a normal rhythm, the mother was given large doses of digoxin every day. I would be doing an ultrasound of the baby later, to ascertain if it was going into heart failure from its prolonged arrhythmia. I would also be checking the mother's blood level of digoxin to make sure that she was not being poisoned from our attempts to help her baby. I was assured by the cardiologist that the mother did not need to be on a heart monitor. The whole thing was a bit of a mystery to me, even with my extensive knowledge of medicine and fluent command of the English language. I could only imagine what this sweet, wispy lady, with limited English, thought we were doing with daily needle sticks, frequent pills and our big ultrasound machine. Later that day, she would ask me, "Is baby okay?" Fortunately, I could tell her "yes."

In those days, pregnant diabetics were admitted to the hospital to figure out how much insulin they needed, to teach them about the diabetic diet and how to inject their insulin. There were a few diabetics on the service. The older patients, in general, were eager to do what had to be done for the baby, but the teenagers were some of the most frustrating patients. Gina, somehow short and lanky at the same time with flat, mousy brown hair, was one of those teenagers and had been in at least four times this pregnancy. I had even shown her a picture of birth defects specific to diabetics, one of which is lack of development of the hip bone. Those children can't even sit. That morning, I found Gina with a king-size Milky Way, half-eaten, in her hand.

Two patients had signs on their doors, "Testing from 2–4 p.m." They were high school students and were taking their final exams in the hospital. One of them had preterm labor and lived in a home with no phone, far from the hospital. Since she could not get help in a reasonable amount of time and could not get to the local clinic for necessary follow-up, she remained in the hospital for several months. The other young woman had been abused at home. The story remained unclear, but the abusing relative, a step-father or uncle, was suspected to be the father of the baby. No one visited her. She was a sweet girl, and the social worker was working hard to find support for her and the baby after the delivery.

As chief resident, I had the prerogative to take the wheeled cart which housed all of the charts. I pushed it from room to room, writing my notes, keeping a list of everything each patient would need for the day, and pretty much forgot that I had had surgery four days ago.

At 7:45 a.m., I was ready to discuss everyone on the antepartum service, patients in the hospital for prenatal complications. Rounds, telling the team of attending physicians about the patients, went smoothly. I knew my patients. The junior residents got most of the hard questions. After rounds, I went to the labor and delivery suite and the outgoing chief resident filled me in on the events of the night. We sat in front of a huge board, with columns for patients' last names, gestational age (how many weeks pregnant), parity (how many babies they had delivered already), last cervical exam (how far dilated), and any special issues. So far, it was a quiet day. Two patients were being induced, one for preeclampsia which was affecting her blood pressure, her liver and kidneys and the blood product, platelets, that controls the blood's ability to clot, and another because she was at term, already four centimeters dilated and lived over an hour away. The intern would probably deliver the latter patient and was in her room talking with her. I was not optimistic that the severe preeclamptic would deliver vaginally before her platelets got so low that her clotting capacity would be effected or before her kidneys were so injured that her body became overloaded with fluid, filling her lungs, making it hard for her to breath. I would be checking on her frequently during the day. There were three regularly laboring patients that the intern would also deliver. One of them was HIV positive, denoted on the large board as "076," after the study just completed which had shown the benefits of treating HIV positive women with AZT in labor.

I discussed the plan with the attending of the day and went to meet the patients. When everyone was "tucked in," the intern, junior resident, attending and I went to get some breakfast at the cafeteria. Just as we were ordering, the intern's pager beeped. "Labor and Delivery, Gotta go," he said, amazingly cheerfully. He must have already eaten.

"I'll bring your breakfast back," I volunteered. I was glad my intern year was over, but I was certain that my eating habits would never be the same. One night, early in my internship year, Steven had come to the hospital to have dinner with me. He patiently waited about 45 minutes, until I could get away to the cafeteria. After we got our food, we sat down and I just shoveled it into my mouth as fast as I could. "Are you okay?" he had asked.

"I just don't know how long I have," I had answered. And, several mouthfuls later, I did have to scurry back to Labor and Delivery for a delivery. After that, he brought dinner to the residents' lounge, partly so that I might have a few extra minutes to eat, but also so that he could be assured of a meal.

After breakfast, I went with the junior resident and the attending to check on the antepartum hospital clinic area, a large, aseptic room where women came for monitoring or amniocentesis. The room had four beds on either side, with a curtain around each bed. The walls were blue and the floor was white. There was nothing playful in the room, not even the curtains. Even when the sun streamed into the windows, it was blocked by the burlap colored curtains, giving the room a somber aura. I wheeled the unwieldy ultrasound machine into the room and to a bed where a diabetic patient was going to have an amniocentesis. We were performing the amniocentesis to test the amniotic fluid for certain chemicals, to see if the lungs were mature enough to deliver the baby. Her sugars had been in very poor control, and we felt that the baby was safer outside than inside, as long as the lungs were mature. The patient knew why she was there, but I reviewed what we were about to do, and why, and what the risks were. I also read a consent form to her, which she then signed. I held the ultrasound over her distended abdomen until I found a good pocket of fluid, a black area on the screen, with no loops of umbilical cord or baby body parts. The junior resident did the actual amniocentesis. The patient would be monitored for about forty-five minutes before going home and the junior resident would call her that night with the results.

By that time, the morning lab work had returned and I walked to the floor to review the results. Nothing unusual. I checked on some diabetic blood sugars and reviewed some monitor strips. Maribelle's baby's heart rate tracing looked a little "flat," but the baby was only 30 weeks. She was the nurse whose baby was not growing well and had IUGR, intrauterine growth restriction. I came back with the ultrasound and the attending to check the baby's movement and breathing patterns, a test called a biophysical profile. We also pushed a button on the machine to check blood flow through the umbilical cord, watching blue and red swishing images of blood flowing through the cord. The baby looked stable today, but she should be given injections of steroids to help the baby's lung to mature. It was likely that she would need to be delivered any day now. She was tearful and frightened. I sat on the side of her bed, held her hand and talked to her for a while. I also had the neonatologist talk to her about babies delivered at 30 weeks and what to expect.

When I got back to Labor and Delivery, I checked Tawana, the preeclamptic patient. She was 15 and this was her first pregnancy, typical for preeclampsia. Before pregnancy, she had been a bit on the chubby side. Now, pregnant and full of fluid, she reminded me of a round water balloon. Her eyes were almost swollen shut from the tissue swelling. Her legs looked like tree trunks and if you pressed your finger in, it left a deep mark for several minutes. I looked at her Foley, the bag draining her bladder. It was empty.

"Did the nurse just empty your Foley," I asked.

Her mother, who was sitting behind me, answered, "The nurse been in, but didn't touch the bag."

"Thank you," I said. "I'll be back in a few minutes."

I sat down at the station with her flow chart and her nurse. Her last blood pressure was very high at 160/110. She had no recorded urine output for the last three hours and had already received a fluid bolus to see if that would make her produce more urine. Her platelets had fallen from 70,000 six hours ago to 40,000. Platelets under 50,000 make you nervous, but people rarely have bleeding problems over 20,000.

I called my attending and, over the phone, recommended a Cesarean section. The patient had received something to soften her cervix two nights ago, been on Pitocin all day yesterday and again had a cervical softening agent last night. She was again on Pitocin, but her cervix still had not dilated at all.

"Does the tracing look all right?" my attending asked.

"Yes, the baby looks fine, but I'm worried about the mother," I answered. I really didn't think it was safe for Tawana to remain pregnant and was afraid that I wouldn't be able to convince my attending to deliver her now. "She hasn't had any urine output for several hours, even after a fluid bolus."

"What are her total fluids for the last 24 and 48 hours? Maybe she is still dehydrated," my attending suggested.

I had the numbers ready. Tawana was ahead on fluids, she had received at least 3 liters more than she had put out over the last 2 days.

"She's only 15," my attending said, indicating that she was still unconvinced that Tawana needed a Cesarean section.

"I know. I hate to have a 15 year old have a uterine incision, but I think this baby needs to come out, sooner rather than later," I pressed.

"Let anesthesia and the nursery know," were the welcome words over the phone.

What a relief. I couldn't wait to be able to make my own decisions.

The junior resident was in clinic that afternoon and there were several impending deliveries for which the intern needed to be available. That meant that I would be doing the Cesarean section with the attending. I called the anesthesiologist and filled her in on Tawana's complications. Since her liver was not in great shape, she would prefer an epidural, but with the platelets so low, an epidural was even riskier. She would want to put in a Swan-Ganz catheter to monitor the fluid status carefully during the surgery and we could use it for the next day or two as well. We decided that it was safest for Tawana to have the surgery under general anesthesia.

I called the blood bank to type and cross match two units of packed red blood cells and to have platelets available should we run into any bleeding problems.

I found the charge nurse and Tawana's nurse to let them know that Tawana would be having a Cesarean section as soon as they were ready. Then, I let the nursery know.

I searched through the files of papers, found a consent form and knocked before going into Tawana's room. She was pretty groggy from the Magnesium Sulfate, a medicine given to preeclamptics to prevent seizures. She seemed to understand that she needed a Cesarean section. I spoke with her mother at length. Because the Cesarean section needed to be done under general anesthesia, her mother would not be allowed to be with her. After reviewing the specifics of the consent form, risks of injury to bowel or bladder, risks of blood transfusion, cardiac arrest or death, I asked Tawana and her mother sign it. I left as the anesthesiologist came in to explain what she was going to do.

Tawana was wheeled down the hall to the operating room and moved onto the operating table. While the anesthesiologist prepped her to place a needle under her collar bone for the Swan Ganz catheter, I put a Doppler on her abdomen to recheck fetal heart tones. The baby sounded good. I reassured Tawana and held her hand while the anesthesiologist numbed her skin, made a small incision with a knife and threaded the catheter under her tiny collar bone.

Then, I left the room to scrub. After putting on a blue paper shower cap, a mask and knee-high paper booties, I looked at my smooth hands, fresh from a week without harsh sponges and betadyne. So long, fair skin. I picked up the plastic nail cleaner and cleaned under all ten nails, then ran the harsh betadyne scrubber under water and scrubbed each finger, all four sides, hands, front and back and arms to the elbows. Just as I was finishing, my attending arrived and began to scrub.

I pushed open the operating room door with my hip and entered with my hands held in the air. Sharina, the scrub tech, gave me a sterile towel to dry my hands, and then helped me push my arms through the sleeves of a blue paper gown and drive my fingers into 2 pairs of sterile gloves. Although younger than I, Sharina had worked in the labor and delivery operating room for years, knew the routine and could get a new intern through anything. She had the loveliest, most reassuring smile, her white teeth contrasting against her black skin, which you couldn't actually see under the OR mask, but, you could see her kindness and competence in her brown eyes, shining behind the plastic eye shields. I thought that her three children were very lucky to have such a competent mother.

"How are you doing, Tawana?" I asked. "It's me, Dr. Levine, under all of this."

"Just scared," she answered.

"You'll be fine," I reassured her. "Soon, you'll be asleep. You may feel some pressure." I added, as I started painting her pregnant abdomen with brown betadyne to sterilize the mound of her belly that would momentarily become the operating field.

When I had finished painting, my attending was ready to help cover Tawana with sterile drapes. I heard the anesthesiologist explaining that we would be putting up a screen to separate her from the sterile field. Beeping in the background indicated that the nursery team had finished setting up the baby warmer and that it was warm enough to receive a baby.

With general anesthesia, the cesarean section is always done as a "STAT," operating as quickly as possible, to get the baby out before the general anesthesia has had a chance to cross the placenta to the baby.

"Ready when you are," I said to the anesthesiologist, holding my scalpel poised for action.

"Go!" she said.

I pressed the scalpel into the now sleeping Tawana, opening her skin, subcutaneous fat, and fascia within seconds. My attending pulled up the next layer, the peritoneum, with a small clamp which I then cut with thin scissors called Metzenbaums before we put our fingers into the hole and pulled on the incision. Next, I cut the layer connecting the bladder to the uterus and pressed the bladder out of the way, protecting the bladder with a retractor ironically called a bladder blade. I put out my hand and, before I could say a word, Sharina handed me a scalpel. I pressed the scalpel gently against the uterus, well aware of the baby's head floating innocently below. I made a few gentle strokes and then pressed the blunt end, the knife handle, into the uterine cavity. With my fingers, I spread the incision. The bag of waters was bulging out and I punctured it with a multi-toothed metal clamp called an Allis clamp.

"Clear fluid," I announced to the nursery team, as I inserted my doubly gloved hand into the open uterus and slid it under the baby's head. My attending pushed from above and the baby's head slipped out. My attending suctioned the baby's nose and mouth while I delivered the remainder of the body, clamped and cut the umbilical cord and handed the baby to the neonatal team. The baby screamed. I took a deep breath.

Reaching my hand back into the uterus, I pressed along the inner edge to disconnect the placenta, which glided off into my hand. Next, we turned our attention to repair of the uterus.

With the baby safely delivered, I could think again. "How long?" I asked.

"Just under two minutes from incision to delivery," the anesthesiologist announced.

My attending smiled, "Good work," he said.

During the C-section, my pager beeped. The nurse who answered it told me that the page was about a consult on the fifth floor.

"Ugh," I groaned. It was always a hassle to do a consult on a non-GYN floor; no matter how hard you tried to anticipate everything that you would need, something was always missing.

After the C-section, I called the nurse's station on the fifth floor. The nurse who answered the phone did not know anything about the patient, and that patient's nurse was "off the floor." She did not know why the other doctor had requested a GYN consult, but was kind enough to look through the chart and tell me that the patient was in her 60's, admitted for congestive heart failure, now doing better, but having a period. "That's too old to be having a period," she added.

"That's probably why they called me," I replied. "Is she stable enough to be brought to the exam room on the GYN floor?" I asked hopefully.

"Yes, but I am not allowed to leave the floor to bring the patient to the GYN floor," she answered. She tried to assure me that they had a GYN bed, complete with stirrups, in their exam room on the fifth floor.

I asked her if she could have a speculum, a light, a pap smear slide, a tenaculum, and endometrial biopsy pipelle and a pair of non-latex gloves in the room.

"I think I can get hold of a speculum," she said.

"That's okay," I answered, realizing that she would never find half of what I needed. "Please, just have a light. Can I meet you and the patient in the room in fifteen minutes?"

"Sure," she said, sounding relieved.

I collected the instruments that I needed, stuffed them all into the pocket of my white coat, and climbed the stairs to the fifth floor. The nurse met me at the door, wheeled the patient inside and vanished.

I stood and talked with the patient, Gretta Smith. Before even beginning the conversation, I could see that she was kind from her pudgy, round, white face, once blond hair, now white, and glistening blue eyes. She looked like the grandmother whose house was "over the river and through the woods." She had never been on hormone replacement therapy and had not bled since her last period over twenty years ago. She was quite heavy and I was pretty sure that she had uterine cancer, or a precursor thereof. Her obesity was actually a comfort to me because, although it is a risk factor for uterine cancer, heavy-set women usually get a much milder uterine cancer than thin women. When she told me that she had not been to a gynecologist or had a pap smear since her last child was born, I became concerned that her bleeding might, instead, be from cervical cancer, which is usually worse than uterine cancer at the stage that it caused bleeding.

I explained that I wanted to do a pap smear as well as a biopsy, which would cause some cramping. I told her that I would go slowly and if anything hurt too much, she should tell me. Some people felt more pain than others with these procedures and if the pain was too much, we could arrange to do everything, even the pap smear, in the operating room with anesthesia.

Mrs. Smith smiled and said, "Honey, I'm sure I can take it. I birthed six babies at home."

I leaned over to help her from the wheelchair to the exam table. While I was supporting her, an almost sharp pain in my belly button incision reminded me that I had had surgery four days ago. With Mrs. Smith successfully on the table, I looked around for a stool. No stool; this was a first, I had never not had a stool.

How could there not be a stool? There was no point searching for the nurse or even searching for a stool. I just squatted where the chair would have been and tried to ignore the discomfort at my incision.

The exam proceeded smoothly and I was able to get both the pap smear and the sampling of uterine tissue. I could often tell just by look and smell if someone had advanced cervical cancer and was relieved that her cervix appeared normal. I helped her back into the wheelchair and explained that we would also be getting an ultrasound to look at her uterus and ovaries. After wheeling her back to her room, I told her that I would check back on her in a few days, but that she, her nurse or her doctor could call me if they needed me sooner, or if her bleeding got heavier. After handing her one of my cards, I pushed the nurse call button to get some help to transfer Mrs. Smith back to bed. By now, my own pelvis was burning.

My pager beeped. It was Labor and Delivery. I called back, and the attending asked if I could come down and help the intern put forceps on, to help a woman who had been pushing for three hours and was completely exhausted.

I did not have time to wait for a nurse. Tick tock. I bent over to help Mrs. Smith out of the wheelchair and onto the bed. She weighed close to 300 pounds and I wished I had one of those weight belts that salesmen wear at hardware stores. She settled easily onto the bed, and was able to bring her own legs up.

I ran down the stairs and exited right into the labor and delivery suite. The intern and the patient were eager for my arrival. She had been pushing for well over three hours and was exhausted. The head was so close, but she just could not muster enough energy for the final thrust. I scrubbed and pulled on a gown and gloves. Booties to protect my shoes would have been nice, but there were none in the room, and they had already been waiting for me for what must have seemed like hours after deciding to give up the pushing efforts. Putting my hand in to test her pelvis, there seemed to be adequate room to easily slide on the smooth, shiny forceps and guide the head out. The baby's head was in the correct position. The patient was comfortable with her epidural. Taking a step back, I coached the intern through testing the position of the head and sliding the forceps in. If they did not slip in easily, then they should not be used. We joked with the patient that the forceps looked like giant salad spoons, as the intern slipped them over the baby's head and gently pulled as the patient pushed. The head slid out, the intern took off the forceps, checked for a cord around the baby's neck, then gently delivered the rest of the body.

The intern had bonded with the family and they were joyfully reviewing the events of the day. I said "Congratulations," and slipped out.

Back at the Labor and Delivery board, it was time for the night team to take over. Unfortunately, tonight, that was me. It was easier than usual, since I already knew the patients. I listened to my junior resident "run the board," relate the plan, patient by patient. She was so poised and confident. I admired her, with a bit of envy.

While things were quiet, the night team had a chance to get dinner from the cafeteria and bring it back to the doctor's lounge. I think we even all got to eat together. It was a busy night with lots of new admissions, deliveries and a C-Section.

Miraculously, around 11 p.m., everyone who needed my attention had delivered and I had answered all of my pages. Lying down in the call room, I instantly fell asleep. A little while later, I felt wet, soaked, in fact. I was really too tired to deal with this and refused to open my eyes. Then, I felt something that I could only describe as a *glub*. "What can be a *glub*?" I thought, still refusing to open my eyes. A blob. A blob can be a *glub*. It was a blob, coming out of me. Reluctantly, I forced my eyes open and turned on the light. My green surgical scrubs were bright red, soaked with blood.

"Damn," I thought, dragging myself out of bed, to the bathroom and into the shower. After my shower, I took my towel and got on my hands and knees to clean off the floor where my shoes and pants had tracked blood. Returning to my call room, I lay back down. Glub, glub; this was not good. I paged my attending, Dr. Green, who went by Susan. A tall, confident brunette whom I had only seen in green scrubs and a white coat, she had had her own share of infertility problems, and I was glad she was the attending that night. I had not shared my plight with her, but felt sure that she would be sympathetic.

When she called back, I picked up the phone and said, "Susan, I hate to bother you. This is Amy. I had a hysteroscopy and laparoscopy four days ago, and I just woke up soaked in blood."

"How much? Have you soaked a pad?"

"You don't want to know. I entirely soaked my pants and the sheets, took a shower and am now sitting on a towel. Do you mind checking me?"

"Meet me in the triage room," she said.

With the towel in my pants, I waddled to the triage room, peeled off my bottoms, put a chux, or super diaper, on the exam table and climbed on. I reached over to the phone on the wall and called Steven. By now, it was about midnight. The only time I had woken him in the middle of the night was right after I had done my first C-Section. The attending had said, "Scalpel to Dr. Levine." I had grasped that scalpel firmly, and proceeded as I had seen others do so many times before. That was a good call, full of excitement and pride. This was not.

"Honey, I'm hemorrhaging," I said calmly. He had been with me through medical school and residency and spoke medicalese as well as any of my colleagues.

"Where are you?" he asked, not nearly as calm as I.

"In the triage room, on Labor and Delivery," I said.

"I'll be right there," he replied. He knew better than to tell me that I should have taken off an extra day or two.

Susan came in with a nurse. (The advantage of being an attending or a guy—you get a nurse.) They both blurted out, "You're awfully pale."

Susan asked the nurse to draw a blood count and blood type, in case I needed a transfusion. Then she sat on the stool, asked me to put my legs in stirrups, adjusted the light and gently slid in a speculum. She quickly pulled it out and wheeled away from the exam table.

"Gushing buckets?" I asked.

"Pretty much," she said. "I think I should call Dr. Taylor." She turned to the nurse, "Anna, would you please start an I.V.?" She had that urgent, "please move quickly, but do not alarm the patient," tone of voice.

It was Dr. Marks who called back. "Sorry to bother you this time of night," Susan began. "I am sitting here with Amy, now four days after her hysteroscopy and laparoscopy. She is bleeding quite briskly." I guessed that she did not want to use the term "hemorrhage," with me in the same room.

Susan nodded a few times and told him that he did not need to come in. She would call back if she needed him. That sounded a bit late to me; I wanted him to come in right away. Susan was a high-risk obstetric specialist. I was an infertility patient with a life-threatening complication, a complication from his surgery and I thought he should be at my side. Of course, I didn't say anything.

Over the phone, he recommended that she put a Foley catheter inside my uterus and leave it inflated.

There was a knock on the door followed by Steven gingerly entering the tiny room. He took one look at me, turned about as pale as I was, and blurted out "Oh, honey!"

"Is she going to be okay?" he asked Susan.

"We just need to stop the bleeding," Susan responded, calmly.

That did not sound good to me, since I knew very well that when uterine bleeding did not stop, the treatment of last resort was a hysterectomy.

When the nurse appeared with a Foley catheter, Steven reminded her that I had a latex allergy. As she headed out for a new Foley, I could still feel the blood pouring out of me. I motioned for Steven to hold my hand. "Hi, Honey," I said cheerfully. "Sorry to wake you. I guess everyone could have had a quiet night, if it weren't for me making such a bloody mess."

"Don't worry about *that*," he and Susan chorused in unison.

"Susan, he's not so good with blood," I said, as I reached for Steven's hand. "He should probably stay up here, near my head."

"I think I can handle things down here," she replied, trying not to sound too concerned.

"Do you think I need to go back to the O.R.?" I asked.

At that moment, the nurse returned with the latex-free Foley and the other instruments Susan would need, including my favorite, the single tooth tenaculum. She slid in the speculum and then I felt the cramp that came with the grasp of the tenaculum. Suddenly, the pain got much worse, as she inflated the bulb of the Foley inside my uterus.

"Are you okay?" she asked. "I need to inflate it quite a bit more. Do you think you need some pain medicine?"

"I have a big case tomorrow," I answered, hoping that I would not have to miss the laparoscopic assisted vaginal hysterectomy that I had scheduled for the next morning. The chief resident on the obstetric service was only allowed to do GYN surgery one day a week, and this was going to be a great case. It combined my favorite surgeries and was with one of my favorite attendings.

"I don't think you're going to be operating tomorrow," Susan laughed. "Go ahead and take the anesthesia."

"All right," I said, and quickly felt a burning in my I.V. as Demerol and Phenergan flowed into my blood stream.

After that, I don't remember too much. I distinctly remember trying to joke with Steven between foggy naps from the narcotics. The junior residents popped in to check up on me. Somehow, I woke up in a Labor room. Susan was reminding me to be sure to thank the Labor and Delivery nurses for letting me stay there and taking care of me. I was not really a labor patient, and they could have insisted that I go to the Emergency Room and then to the GYN floor. Yes, thank you for reminding me that I have not achieved labor status, let alone pregnancy. In any case, I must have stopped bleeding, since no one mentioned a hysterectomy. I put my hand where the incision would have been, and was relieved to find the skin still intact. Over the course of the morning, I checked several times, since the pain medicine interfered with my memory, and I was never too sure that I had not had a hysterectomy.

"As soon as the Demerol has cleared enough for you to walk, you can go home," Susan told me. "Dr. Marks wants you to stay in bed with the Foley in until Friday."

"Wow," I said. "But, I'm on call Thursday."

Then I noticed that Janis, the resident who had put in the laminaria, had come in with Susan. "Don't worry about that. we'll cover it," Janis said.

"Janis," I said, trying to sit up, "I have an LAVH at 10:30. Do you want it?"

"They've already given it to Anne," she answered.

"I really wanted you to have it," I responded. "Who is going to have to be OB chief?" It was one of the most grueling rotations, not one on which any of us wanted to spend extra time.

"I think they're bringing Jim back from elective." Janis looked at her watch. "I hope you feel better. I've got to get to clinic. Let me know if I can do anything."

"Thanks," I said. "Actually, there is. Last night, I saw a Mrs. Smith on the fifth floor. She has post menopausal bleeding. I did a pap and endometrial biopsy. She should be having an ultrasound today. If you could have someone check on her for me that would be great."

Janis wrote down the name and room number. "I'll pass it along to the oncology chief," she said.

Well, that conversation had pretty much exhausted me. "Let's get out of here," I said to Steven, who was sitting next to me, still looking worse than I felt. Of course, I felt pretty good with the Demerol.

In the car on the way home, I asked, "Did I get a blood transfusion?"

"No," Steven said, laughing.

"What's so funny?" I asked, glad to see him smile.

"First, you're still slurring your words and second, you've asked me that almost every five minutes," he answered.

"And, every time, it's good news," I responded.

"Yes, every time."

Steven helped me up the stairs and tucked me into bed. I kept checking my belly for scars, just to make sure that I had not had a hysterectomy. No scars, at least on the outside.

CHAPTER 7

▼

A QUICKIE

Since my little bleeding incident, everyone knew that I was trying to get pregnant. Everyone knew that I was failing at getting pregnant. And, everyone probably knew that I had a freak uterus. Presumably, since the surgery, it looked okay. I remembered that when we heard that Stacey had breast cancer, we all looked at her mammogram. We looked at it out of concern, but now I wondered if perhaps she had not wanted everyone to see inside of her body. To this day, I have a blazing image of that horrible, spiculated breast mass that would eventually kill her. When I talked to her on the phone, in addition to picturing her face, I could not erase the image of that menacing mass. Maybe the residents would be too busy to check my HSG. Maybe, I would not end up as the subject of rounds that morning.

HSG. Yes, I would need another HSG. Even though I had not needed a hysterectomy, it was still quite possible that all of the bleeding and keeping a Foley in for a week would scar the lining of my uterus, making it impossible for me to have children. Putting my hand on my belly could not reassure me about what was going on inside of my uterus. I prayed open thoughts, "Do not close up," I chanted to myself, as I rubbed the area which had been spared a hysterectomy scar.

I had a wonderfully uneventful week in bed: the vacation I needed.

And, I missed being on call for the most catastrophic event of the year.

It was the Thursday night that would have been my night on call. One of the junior residents signed out a patient to the second year resident, but he should have signed her out to the intern (first year resident.) When the intern got a call that the patient's urine output was low, he ordered some fluids, a very routine post operative event. Since patients are not allowed to eat the night before surgery, they are often dehydrated and have low urine output after surgery. A bit later, the intern was called again. This time, the patient's pulse was up and blood pressure was down. The urine output still almost zero. The intern immediately went to see the patient, looked through the chart and called the attending who had done the case. The intern also called the chief resident, who got everything ready so that the patient, who was clearly bleeding internally, was in the operating room by the time the attending arrived. When they could not find the source of bleeding, they called in the GYN oncologist who found and stopped the bleeding. The patient was a Jehovah's Witness and her family refused to allow her to have a blood transfusion. So, instead of bouncing back quickly, she had to be in the intensive care unit under close surveillance for several weeks. Somehow, even though the chief resident on call was not the original surgeon on the case nor the person called for the initial low urine output, nor the person who had been told about the case in the first place, the chief on call that night was held most accountable. Better to be home in bed with a Foley catheter in your uterus!

While lying in bed, I came to terms with the fact that everyone definitely knew that I was trying to get pregnant. It was late enough in the year that a pregnancy would not affect them. I would be finished with residency months before I would need maternity leave, that ultimate betrayal of your peers.

After the bleeding fiasco, I had to take two months off from trying to get pregnant while my biologic clock ticked on, tick, tock, tick, tock. You really feel like an idiot using a condom when you are not only hopelessly infertile and not ovulating, but want to be pregnant more than anything in the world. And, to add insult to injury, because of my latex allergy, I had to buy sheepskin condoms that were always hidden at the pharmacy and cost several times what normal condoms for normal people cost.

Finally, it was time to try again. This time, I wrote my own prescription for Clomid. Of course, my ovulation kit turned positive on a morning that I had to be in the hospital so early that there was no way I could lie in bed after sex, let alone have sex. Maybe the little guys would be strong enough to swim up hill. I certainly had heard of teenagers standing up and douching with Coca Cola after intercourse, and they still got pregnant. But, I knew that would not be me.

Instead, I took a chance by waiting for the evening. Around 4 p.m., I asked my junior resident, Allie, if she could cover for me for an hour or two when the night shift started. Allie, always calm in an emergency, and never overwhelmed by the work at hand, was a beautiful, tall, slim, light skinned black woman who had gone to the University of Pennsylvania for both undergraduate and medical school, and came from a family of doctors.

She looked at me quizzically. I have never been good at making up stories, and I figured everyone knew that I was trying to get pregnant, anyway. I took a deep breath and forced myself to explain. "I took Clomid this cycle and today was the two blue lines. I don't want to miss it." That was about as discreet as I could be. For some reason, I did not want to say the word ovulate. I should have just said that I needed to go home and have sex, that tonight was really not a convenient night to work.

We were both well aware of an article in the New England Journal a few months before which had implied that more than 12 months of Clomid might increase your risk of ovarian cancer. As residents, we easily attacked the study, how it was done, what other reasons that there might be for the ovarian cancer. But, as someone taking Clomid, I did not care what was wrong with the study. I just wanted to know how many months were safe.

"No problem," she said. Then added, "Don't rush. We'll be fine. And, don't worry. I'll tell them you had to pick someone up at the airport, or something."

Steven met me at home. I could not say that it was our most romantic moment. Totally stressed about leaving the hospital, certain that some disaster would happen and no chief resident would be there, I checked my pager every fifteen minutes to make sure it was working. Fortunately, Steven was up to the challenge.

After the fact, as I lay with my bottom propped on a pillow, I debated with myself how long to stay home. I did not want to take advantage of my junior resident's kindness to cover for me, but I did not want her to think that I (we) had rushed through our intimate moments or that the whole thing had only taken twenty minutes. Fifteen minutes of lying still and worrying were about all I could take. Jumping out of bed, I pulled on clean undies, a new underwire, white cotton bra and my green hospital scrubs and clogs, and kissed Steven's sweetly relaxed, slightly scruffy late afternoon shadow.

"Can I drive you back?" he offered, sounding more than half asleep.

"Not to worry," I called back, heading out the door.

It was a crazy night, racing from emergency to emergency, with multiple trips to the operating room. Between Cesarean sections for fetal distress, I operated on two women with ectopic pregnancies, pregnancies in the fallopian tube. Both women had come in with pelvic pain. The first, a heavy-set red head, twenty years old, had come in with her mother. On admission, she had been stable, just complaining of pain, and had been surprised to find out that she was pregnant, and then even more surprised to find out that not only was the pregnancy in the wrong place, it would have to be removed surgically immediately. I had Tim, the junior resident who had seen my HSG, explain the surgery to her and her mother. We would be able to do it through the laparoscope, only making a small incision in her belly button and a few more small incisions near her bikini line. She and her mother, model images of each other twenty years apart, just stared at Tim. He was the good-looking athletic type that usually goes into orthopedics, but he was great with the sensitive OB/GYN issues.

Shortly after Tim and I completed this surgery, without mentioning my insides or the fact that I had been missing in action at the beginning of the shift, the emergency room nurse paged me again. An ambulance was arriving with a patient who had already lost consciousness. All we knew was that a few days ago, the patient had told her mother that she had a positive pregnancy test. Earlier in the evening, she had complained of severe lower abdominal pain. Her mother had heard a thud from the bathroom as her daughter collapsed on the bathroom floor.

The paramedics had started two large I.V. lines. They told us that the mother had signed a consent for treatment, but stayed home with the other children. "House was a real mess," one of the paramedics continued, amazingly calm, with his blue eyes reflected in his blue uniform and his name, "Harold," in bold yellow letters. "Kids everywhere. One still nursing. Poor mom had almost no teeth left."

We had an operating room ready when she arrived. Tim, always the dextrous athlete, scanned her thin, white abdomen with the ultrasound as we headed down the hall to the operating room, confirming that the inside of her belly was full of blood. We could not see much of her face, as the paramedics held an oxygen mask in place. Thick, long brown hair was matted under her head. We wheeled her into the operating room, stopping to don our hats, masks and boots, as the anesthesia resident continued with the stretcher into the O.R.

I rapidly prepped and draped her, cut through skin, thick subcutaneous fat, and the fascia and entered the inner space full of blood. After quite a bit of suctioning, we located one "pumper," the blood vessel that was responsible for most of the blood loss. After tying off the vessel actively squirting blood, we located the pregnancy tissue, removed it from the fallopian tube and were able to save the fallopian tube.

As we were closing, my pager went off again. The circulating nurse picked up the pager and read the numbers, "2440–911." STAT to Labor and Delivery. Quickly pulling off my surgical gown and gloves, I left Tim to finish with the gynecology attending, who happened to be Dr. Taylor that night, wondering if they would talk about me during the quiet part of the case, when they were just closing the patient.

I ran up the stairs to find the intern, Jim, in the triage room, standing with the ultrasound machine next to a woman lying on the exam table in a pool of blood.

Always the Southern gentleman, he introduced me in his slight, but definite, Southern accent. "Shanaya, this is Dr. Levine, the chief resident here tonight. She will be helping to take care of you and your baby."

Shanaya had very wrinkled, aged brown skin, although only in her mid-thirties. She was very thin, with dark brown eyes, sweat beaded on her forehead, and track marks showing on her arms, under the thin, yellow hospital gown. Her abdomen was rock hard, a Couvelaire uterus, a sign of a placental abruption or separation. "The baby still has a heart beat," Jim panted, as we wheeled her rapidly to the cesarean section room.

"Please don't hit me, ma'm," Jim requested, calmly. He stood six feet tall, had wonderfully thick blond hair, blue eyes and found time to work out every day that he was not on call and managed residency, a wife and two children with apparent ease. His hand deftly caught Shanaya's in mid-air.

She yelled and screamed, "Don't take my baby," as we tried to explain that the placenta, the baby's blood supply had separated from the wall of the uterus and that her baby could die quickly if we did not deliver it. "Please save my baby! Don't take my baby from me! I'm sorry. I'm sorry. I won't do it no more!" I had the nurse draw urine from the Foley for a drug screen before narcotics were given. We hardly needed confirmation that crack or cocaine had caused this abruption. She screamed over and over as we wheeled her down the hall, transferred her to the operating room table and as the intern started her I.V. "Save my baby! Don't let them take my baby from me! I want my baby!"

Rapidly, we prepped her belly with betadyne, draped her, and suddenly it was quiet. Jim concentrated intently, holding the scalpel with great assurance. "One cut, straight to the fascia," I coached.

"Two minutes," I said, as he pulled the baby out. "Great work."

Of course, I did not get pregnant that night. What kind of baby would want to grow in a body with that kind of stress?

A few weeks later, the junior residents threw a party and roast for the outgoing chief residents. When they got to me, the emcee started by saying, "Amy, we're so glad you could make it tonight. We were afraid you might be ovulating."

I looked at Steven, certain that he would be upset. He was a very private person, especially about private things, but he was laughing. I forced a laugh. Wow. Hanging out with OB/GYN residents for four years had steeled him to almost anything. Not me. I wanted to lock myself in the bathroom and cry.

CHAPTER 8

▼

SCHEDULING CYCLES

The end of residency was in sight. I used my remaining vacation time to fly to Atlanta for interviews. My Ivy League resume got me in the door; the rest was up to me. Four years of stress and sleep deprivation had definitely improved my charm and personality.

At one interview, I watched while an ultrasound technician performed an ultrasound on twins. The father-to-be was a truck driver, a friendly, burly guy with his name, Harlan, on his shirt. As the technician discussed the many body parts on the screen, Harlan, with his deep, strong voice, light-heartedly, but with real concern, joked about the tremendous expense of two babies at once. The couple was so happy; I almost cried from jealousy and the unfairness of it all. In residency, I didn't have to see happy, healthy couples having happy, healthy babies. It was easy to distance myself from the crack-addict teenagers.

In my job interviews, I let every one know that I planned to get pregnant as soon as possible. Even though prospective employers weren't allowed to ask specifically about having children, these doctors were OB/GYNs, and I was clearly at *that* age and not getting younger. You could just look at me and hear my biological clock going "tick, tock." As I asked about maternity leave, I wondered if I was losing good jobs over a maternity leave that I might never need. Maybe, I'd be a more attractive candidate if I just told them that I was infertile. I couldn't imagine "real life" and a "real job."

In the last five minutes of residency, as I was signing out the Labor and Delivery patients to Allie, now chief on the obstetric service, Tim ran into the room. "The patient in room four just complained of shortness of breath and passed out. The anesthesia resident is intubating." We all knew that it was most likely, an amniotic fluid embolism, a condition that is fatal 80% of the time. As I started to run to room four, Allie gently, and calmly, pulled me back.

"I've got it," she said. "Go home. You've earned it. Tim, page Dr. Stills, tell him we're doing a section. Then meet me in the back. You're doing the case." Wow. I was done.

Once I started my "real job," I got back to the business of trying to get pregnant. Dr. Taylor had given me the name of a friend and colleague of his in Atlanta, Dr. Bonderant. After one more month of self-prescribed Clomid did not work, I called. I told him my story, and added that I was on day 12 of my cycle.

Well, a fertility doctor can't stand to miss a cycle, and he asked if I could come that afternoon.

As luck would have it, I was on call. So, I asked my new employer, Dr. Halle, if he could cover for me for an hour or two that afternoon. Dr. Halle was tall with reddish brown hair, laughing brown eyes, an easy smile and always wore suits that hung a bit on his tall, thin body. He only wore a white coat if he was wearing scrubs. Otherwise he wore his full suit, often toying with the buttons, but, finally, leaving them open. His ties, all fine silk, were clearly picked by his wife.

"Are you pregnant?" he asked with a mischievous smile, implying that he would be happy for me if I was.

"The opposite," I replied, trying for humor. "Dr. Bonderant said he could see me today."

"Dr. Bonderant? He has a six month waiting list," said Dr. Halle.

"Well, I just called him. I did mention that it was day 12 of my cycle."

"You can't miss an appointment with him. You may never get another. You must have some pretty serious connections," Dr. Halle chuckled. "Sure, I'll cover for you. Good luck."

I called Steven and he said that he could meet me there.

Welcome to the world of private infertility clinics. The office was in a building nicknamed "The Gucci Building." It had a green mirrored facade, with an elegant, striped pattern. There were no hard, plastic chairs or white and black tiled floors here. The office had a huge waiting room, with a lush green carpet, prints of Impressionist paintings in gold-leaf frames on the walls, living room-style armchairs, several telephones for patients to use, and elegant, sparkly clean bathrooms located right next to the waiting room. Each doctor had a window with their own receptionist.

I walked to Dr. Bonderant's receptionist's window. As I was picking up the pen to sign in, a friendly voice on the other side said, "You must be Dr. Levine. Dr. Bonderant told me you would be coming. I'm Melissa. I make all of his appointments."

"Nice to meet you, Melissa," I answered. This was a powerful woman, in charge of a six month waiting list. In fact, it would be much harder for me to bypass her in the future.

I sat down in a plush, green paisley armchair, and picked up that month's issue of The New Yorker. Anxiously, I flipped through the cartoons, which were not sufficient to distract me. Fortunately, Steven walked in at that moment and I waved.

"Quite an operation," he laughed, his eyes scanning the opulent setting and skyline view from the large, perfectly clean windows.

In a few moments, a prim, young black woman, with beautiful, dark skin, a zillion tiny braids held neatly in a bun, and wearing a pressed, aqua scrub suit called my name. After introducing herself in a very proper-sounding English accent as "Elizabeth, Dr. Bonderant' s nurse," she led Steven and me through a maze of hallways to an elegant wooden door with a shiny brass name plate which read "Dr. Bonderant" in upright, bold letters. She knocked on the door, and, a moment later, Dr. Bonderant opened the door.

Elizabeth introduced us, as if we were meeting at a dinner party. Her English accent and all of the wood paneling made me feel as if we were at Buckingham Palace.

Dr. Bonderant gave us a very white polished, but genuine, smile and invited us into his office, which could have been the inspiration for the over-used phrase "well-appointed." Steven and I sank into the arm chairs, and Dr. Bonderant sat on the other side of his solid mahogany desk in a large, leather chair that tilted back, allowing him to assume an informal pose while maintaining command of the room. He had kind brown eyes and a full head of dark brown hair. His suit, a blue summer-weight wool had been on the cover of the Paul Stuart catalogue, with the same tie.

He started with chit-chat, about Steven's job and mine, what had brought us to Atlanta. He seemed a little surprised that I was with Dr. Halle's group, but I attributed that to their suburban location. He told us about his background, and that he had trained with Dr. Taylor. That brought the conversation neatly to the matter at hand, my infertility and my being on day 12. He suggested that I come to the office after I ovulated, for a postcoital test, to make sure that Steven's sperm were swimming in my cervical mucus. I explained that I was on call this weekend, but would try to make it. He wrote down the phone number that I was to call if I ovulated over the weekend. He explained, at length, the weekend call schedule, what to say when I called and what would happen when I came in.

"What if it's fine?" I asked. I knew that if it was not fine, the next step would be intrauterine insemination (IUI).

"I think it's important to know," he answered. "In any case, I'd also like you to come back about ten days after you ovulate to do an endometrial biopsy, to make sure that you don't have a luteal phase defect."

I refrained from asking if I could just do an IUI this month. I was not interested in a fact finding mission; I just wanted a baby. I agreed, however, that the endometrial biopsy was a good idea. After all, he was the big expert.

He led Steven and me into an exam room, and Elizabeth magically appeared to give me instructions. Dr. Bonderant came back a few minutes later, and did a culture for Chlamydia. Chlamydia can cause an infection and block your tubes, even without causing any symptoms. Of course, we already knew that my tubes were open from the HSG. I was trying hard to be the patient and not the doctor, so I just nodded.

When we were finished, he wished me luck, scribbled some things on a paper and stepped out of the room. I had just finished dressing when Elizabeth knocked. In her lovely English accent, she reviewed the details of the post-coital test, that after my ovulation kit was positive, we should have sex and then come to the office no more than six hours later. She also had the bad job of explaining that the paper on the counter was the bill and that I should take it to the check out counter, a few hallways away. Payment was due at the time of service. When she asked if I had any questions, I marveled at how polite and unhurried she was. It was late on a Friday afternoon; her scrub suit still looked neatly pressed, and not a wisp of hair had come out of her bun.

As soon as she stepped out of the room, I grabbed the bill, eager to see how the cash world of infertility compared with the managed care world where I worked. "I definitely should have done a fellowship," I quipped to Steven.

We made our way to the check-out counter. Miraculously, they were on my insurance plan, and I only paid some small co-pay.

Private practice was like a vacation compared to residency and I was able to return on Sunday for a postcoital test, without having to call any of my partners to cover for me and explain that I was ovulating.

I had slept in the hospital Saturday night, after a 2 a.m. delivery. I got an early start on rounds and called Steven at 8 a.m. to tell him that I was on my way home and that today was the day. I was relieved to have ovulated on a Sunday, because I had not figured out how I would have gotten out of the office on Monday. I could not very well just show up late, and getting out of the office before the six-hour window closed on the sperm could have been tricky.

Fortunately, we were uninterrupted by my pager and even had time for a few kisses before getting down to business. I called the number Dr. Bonderant had given me, and the nurse on the other end said that they would be expecting me shortly. We hopped in the car and drove to the Gucci Building. I felt as if everything was dripping out of me. Well, we would soon see.

That morning, the waiting room had quite a few people in it, but the receptionists' windows were closed. There was a sign-in sheet next to the Poland Springs water fountain. After flipping the attached gold Cross pen in place, I signed in. Looking around, but trying not to stare, I wondered who else was there to have their sexual prowess checked. No one, including me, radiated anything that I would call a postcoital glow.

Within a few moments, someone in pressed scrubs called my name. Steven and I rose from our seats and followed her down a hallway. "You're here for a Huhner's test?" she asked discreetly, when we were out of earshot of the waiting room.

"Mmhmm," I answered, nodding affirmatively. This was serious business. The nurse did not grin nor smirk, but the whole thing struck me as rather funny, at that moment.

She led us to an exam room and gave me a sheet to drape over my legs, then stepped out, closing the door with a solid click. I shimmied off my bottoms and sat on the table. A young woman with the name Dr. Amblee on her white coat entered the room. She looked younger than I, with flowing brunette hair that had definitely been curled and blow dried that morning. Her make up was in subtle tones, but clearly there, with mauve eye shadow, black eye-liner, a tannish base, a light pink blush and a liquor colored lipstick. She introduced herself and confirmed that I was there for a Huhner's or post coital test. She asked when I had ovulated, how long ago we had intercourse and when we had intercourse the time before that. Dutifully, she recorded all of this in blanks on a piece of paper in my chart. Then, she pulled the stirrups out of the exam table and asked me to lie back. I put my feet in the stirrups and scooted to the end of the table. She deftly inserted a speculum, withdrew fluid from my cervix and vagina, squirted them onto glass slides and removed the speculum.

"Would you like to look at it?" she asked.

"Oh, yes," I replied, glad to return from my position as a vagina full of semen to a respected colleague.

As I was getting dressed, Steven commented, "That really did look like a turkey baster."

"Do you want to come to the lab with me?" I asked him, admiring his consistency in his khaki shorts, blue polo shirt and penny loafers with pennies but no socks.

"No, you can give me the report. I'll wait here."

I quickly dressed and a kind-looking nurse I had not seen before pointed me toward the lab. Of course, Steven's little guys were still swimming with aim and purpose in the correct direction. That also meant that I had passed my part of the test. My cervical mucous worked. Hallelujah!

With ten days warning, I was less stressed about making arrangements to be out of the office to drive across town to have my uterus biopsied. When I asked to take a half of a vacation day on a Thursday afternoon, no one asked why. That was easy. Getting the appointment for Thursday afternoon was not so easy, but eventually I cajoled Melissa into slipping me into Dr. Bonderant's schedule.

The endometrial biopsy was not fun. Since there was a chance that I might be pregnant, I didn't want to take any pain medication. Sometimes, people get pregnant just from making the appointment with the fertility specialist. Psychologically, it relieves them of the responsibility and they're able to relax and get pregnant. Maybe, that would be me. Just in case, I didn't want to take any Tylenol or Motrin. I knew very well those medicines were perfectly safe this early. Even if I were to be pregnant that month, the embryo would barely have implanted and would not have been exposed to the medicine. Still, you can never be too safe.

I tried to read a few articles in the waiting room before being led to an exam room and given a sheet. I slipped off my bottoms, donned the sheet and sat up, waiting to see who would come in. Dr. Bonderant knocked and came in, most cheerful for the end of the day. He expressed genuine delight at the excellent post-coital test and asked if I was ready for the biopsy. I grimaced and lay back down on the table. Elizabeth, again, magically appeared beside him. As I lay back on the table, I focused on Elizabeth's braids, freely flowing down her back.

After being impressed with how smoothly he slipped in the speculum, I felt the crunch of my too familiar friend, the tenaculum, on my cervix. "Amy," he said sweetly, "I am going to have to dilate you."

"Even after the hysteroscopy and two HSG's?" I asked.

"Your cervix has closed right back up," he answered.

"Whatever you have to do," I said. "I wonder if it's keeping the little guys from swimming up there." I tried to count Elizabeth's many, many shiny braids.

"Could be," he said, gently pressing the smooth, metal dilators into my slammed shut cervix.

It turned out that what I had told my patients was true: you basically only feel cramping down there. Cramping from the speculum, cramping from the tenaculum and cramping from the dilator. Then, YOUCH! Gigantic cramping from the biopsy pipelle, an innocent looking long, thin plastic tube with a built-in suction function.

"Are you okay?" Dr. Bonderant asked with concern.

"Fine," I answered. I thought I was very stoic, barely flinching, but I guess I had not been quite as tough a cookie as I thought. And, of course, I bled a bit more than he had expected. I was certain that whatever clot had broken off after my hysteroscopy and caused me to hemorrhage had broken off again. I did not want to spend another week in bed with a Foley in my uterus. I was lying there, imagining myself at work with a Foley in my uterus, the catheter tucked in my pantyhose and the bag tied to my knee under a skirt, when Dr. Bonderant assured me that everything looked fine.

After stopping by the clerk, a matter-of-fact looking, middle aged woman, also in pressed scrubs, at the check out desk and paying my co-pay, I reminded myself that sometimes women get pregnant the month of their endometrial biopsy. The biopsy makes a divette in the uterine lining for the embryo. It snuggles in there like an egg in a nest.

As usual, no nice little embryo was snuggling in my nest that month. My period arrived, exactly 14 days after I ovulated. No mercy. Not even a day late so that, at least for a day, I could hope.

CHAPTER 9

▼

THE FOUR-DAY WEEKEND

No sooner had I seen that first drop of blood of my period than I called Dr. Bonderant, telling him that I needed an IUI the next month. He agreed. His plan was that I should take Clomid and then a hormone injection of beta HCG, the pregnancy hormone, to stimulate ovulation.

Looking at the calendar, I noticed that several months had slipped by and Thanksgiving would be right around ovulation. Dr. Bonderant assured me that they were open on Thanksgiving. There were no holidays in the fertility business. With dismay, I noted that I was on call the entire four days of Thanksgiving weekend.

I casually asked around the office the next day, to find out which doctors would be home over the holiday weekend. As it turned out, one partner, Paul, whose wife had been through infertility treatments, would be in town and he was happy to cover for me. Prematurely gray but with a full head of hair, Paul had an out-doorsman style friendliness. I assured him that the procedure should not take long and certainly could be arranged not to interfere with Thanksgiving dinner.

Steven and I had a nice, quiet Thanksgiving dinner together. I had made rounds earlier in the day and since no one was in labor, I went home. We had a great time, preparing our favorite dishes and a new soup in a pumpkin, with toasted brochette and cheese. We made a soup-filled pumpkin for each of us and had enough food to have invited all of the neighbors that we didn't know, which was all of them.

Later that night, before I went back to the hospital for a delivery, Steven gave me my beta HCG shot. The delivery ended up as a C-section, around 2 in the morning, with a ten pound four ounce baby boy and two very happy, very proud and very tired parents.

When I called Paul at nine in the morning to tell him that I had to go in for my "appointment" no one was in labor, and I had finished rounds. I debated not calling him at all, so I would not have to bother him. But, if someone arrived at the hospital without calling, I did not want to have to fly off of the table with a speculum still inside of me, speeding across town. It was not a pretty image. Also, I thought the procedure might work better if I could relax.

Steven drove me to the Gucci Building. Then he went off to the room with the plastic couches and magazines. I believe they now have videos or DVD's, but this was a long time ago. I did not realize that it took a little while to process the sperm, and immediately worried that Paul would have to cover for me for too long. Steven reassured me that it was not Thanksgiving any more and nothing had been going on when I left. "I'm sure he's sitting at home with his family, having a nice quiet day," Steven said.

Finally, a nurse called my name and Steven and I followed her down a different set of hallways. The exam room looked exactly the same as the others and I did exactly the same thing that I had done in the others: took off my bottoms, draped a sheet over myself and sat on the table. The knock on the door was followed by a very young woman in a doctor's coat entering the room. She was wearing black silk pants, black high heeled shoes, open at the toe and heel, and a bright pink silk shirt under her white coat. She had gold hearts dangling from each ear. A very senior looking nurse with bifocals, wearing scrubs and a white coat, accompanied her. After introducing herself, Dr. Solo, and the nurse, Mrs. Fitzgerald, she looked at my chart and said, "Gee, I hope you don't need to be dilated again."

I wondered if she was a resident, moonlighting. Since I certainly did not want to know if she was, I did not ask. What year resident? Had she ever dilated a cervix? You could perforate, or make a hole in, the uterus dilating a cervix. I had done that in training and had been devastated. A simple procedure had turned into a blood bath. Fortunately, I knew immediately what had happened. It was not hard to tell that the blood pouring out of the vagina should not have been there. I called a senior resident who called an attending and we took the patient to the operating room and everything turned out all right. Long after the patient had fully recovered, I was still traumatized. Well, now it's my turn, I figured, as I lay back on the table, putting my feet up in stirrups.

The woman seemed to be fumbling around and was not nearly as suave with the speculum as Dr. Bonderant, or as I hoped I was, for that matter.

"You do need to be dilated," the young woman in the doctor's coat sighed. "I hope I don't perforate," she muttered to herself.

"I hope you don't, also," I prayed silently.

I heard Mrs. Fitzgerald whisper to Dr. Solo as she handed her a syringe with a long catheter attached, cautioning her not to spill it. If she had sounded as if she were joking, I would have felt better. Had she dropped the last syringe?

I squeezed Steven's hand. He was watching the doctor and nurse team intently. "Don't let them drop it," I wanted to shout. The tip of the catheter had to remain sterile, since it was going into my cervix. Maybe not totally sterile, but, hopefully, more sterile than the floor.

Feeling my uterus cramp was actually a most welcome cramp, because it meant that Dr. Solo, whom I was now certain was a resident, had actually managed to insert the catheter through my cervix and into my uterus. When she was finished, she said that it did not matter if I stayed lying down or not, but that I was welcome to stay in the room. I thanked her and as soon as she left, I took the pillow from underneath my head and tucked it under my bottom.

While I was lying with my bottom propped up, I called Paul to see what was going on. I pictured him in his living room, the sun streaming through the sheer curtains over the bay windows; his wife and one year old daughter, playing on the floor. His voice was comforting. "Nothing is going on. Not even one call."

I told him that I would call the answering service and have them direct the calls back to me. "Thanks for covering," I added.

"It was nothing," he answered.

Well, I had used up a favor, but at least I had not had to ask permission to go home and have sex! There was at least one advantage of a more technical conception.

Saturday, I drove back and forth between two hospitals, with women in labor at both. Every night of that Thanksgiving weekend, Thursday, Friday, Saturday and Sunday I had to do at least one C-Section between one and four in the morning. By the time I got home after office hours on Monday, I was wiped out. If Steven and I ever had a child, it would be bright. No child of ours would be dumb enough to sign on with a body that was up for four nights in a row doing C-Sections. I could not blame the little egg and sperm for escaping that month.

When I called Dr. Bonderant after my next period, he wanted to do another test, painless, at least physically. Steven needed to give another sample, and I needed to give a blood sample. They would run his little guys past my blood to see if I had antibodies to them, to see if I had cells in my blood that attacked his sperm, like torpedoes on a mission.

My last few tests had gone pretty well; my repeat HSG had been normal, my endometrial biopsy had shown that my uterine cells were doing their job to support a pregnancy should one choose to land there; my cervical mucous had allowed the sperm to swim. I was on a roll, passing every test. Sure, I would put myself on the line again, see how my body performed.

When the nurse tried to draw my blood, nothing came out the first time. As a runner, I happen to have excellent veins, but the nurse was immediately on the offensive, accusing me of not having had enough to drink that morning, causing my veins to be small, making her job of drawing my blood more difficult. Eventually, she got the blood that she needed, but I already knew that my body had stopped cooperating; I would not be passing this test.

Without any apparent complication, and with no comment to me about any details, Steven gave his sample. As we drove home, I pressed the cotton ball to the still smarting place in the crook of my elbow that had refused to yield blood to the nurse.

Dr. Bonderant called me that evening. I pictured him in his wood paneled office, sitting behind his sturdy, shiny desk, wearing an Italian designer tailored, summer wool, gray suit, the cheerful smile that he always seemed to have lighting up the room, leaning back in his chair, maybe with his feet in their black polished shoes resting on the corner of the desk. "Guess what?" he said, cheerfully. "You have antisperm antibodies."

"But my Huhner's test was okay," I said. "The little guys were swimming in my cervical mucus."

"The antibodies can live in the fallopian tubes," he explained.

"So, there's no point in doing another IUI?" I asked, trying to assemble my facts quickly.

"I think we should try one more month," he answered with the kindness but firmness of someone who had done this many times.

When I was in residency, the fertility department "did not believe in" antisperm antibodies. A visiting junior resident had once given a talk on antisperm antibodies. I had been sitting next to him, watching him get more and more uncomfortable, sweat beads forming on his forehead, as the attending questioned him, repeatedly refuting the existence of antisperm antibodies. As Dr. Bonderant talked, I tried hard to remember why antisperm antibodies might or might not exist, but in the end, it did not matter; I had them.

I tried to figure out when my body would have created these attacker cells, these antisperm antibodies. Unlike a uterine septum, I had not been born with antibodies to my husband's sperm; my immune system had to develop them. At some point, his sperm had crossed into my blood stream, causing my body to make antibodies, as if they were foreign bacteria. Once, before I knew that I had an allergy, we had used a latex condom, trying to do the right thing. Responsible young professional that I was, after missing two birth control pills, I was being careful, using a backup method, just like I advised my patients. Most of my patients did not listen to, or did not remember at the necessary moment of passion, my warning to use back up contraception, and they got pregnant. I should have been so lucky! Instead of getting pregnant and having a beautiful baby, I did the responsible thing, used condoms and ended up with the most painful burning sensation in an area where no one should have painful burning.

Dr. Bonderant continued talking about the next stage of treatment, but questions were flying through my mind. Since the egg and sperm met in the fallopian tube, and mine had venomous antisperm antibodies lurking in its crevices, what was the point of an IUI, which still entailed the sperm making its way through my poisoned fallopian tubes?

Dr. Bonderant continued, "I think it's worth one more try. Especially, if you can avoid IVF." In vitro fertilization, referred to by those who do it daily as IVF, was the last step that might allow us to have our own child, and involved probably hundreds of injections, the painful, deep-in-the-muscle kind, sometimes daily appointments for ultrasounds and blood tests, and much, much more money. At that moment, he was probably looking at the family picture on his desk. It was a picture of the whole family in Switzerland, all wearing, what had looked to me like, very expensive ski outfits. That was paid for by IVF's.

"Same protocol?" I asked. Although I was sure that I would need IVF, I suddenly realized that the demands of IVF would challenge my office schedule and mean asking for quite a bit of time off from my new practice. "Please make the IUI work," I prayed.

"Yes," he answered.

"Can I get an older doctor to do the next IUI?" I asked, trying to sound light hearted.

"Sure," he laughed, but did not ask for details.

When I told Steven that I had antisperm antibodies, I could almost see into his brain as he he caught the gist of it immediately. "You're killing my guys," he laughed, pulling me in with his strong tennis arms for a much needed hug. Forget all the fancy immunology theories, forget about trying to figure out when his sperm had been exposed to my blood stream so that I made antibodies, and forget the academic question of whether or not they existed. In a nutshell, I was killing his guys.

I don't remember much about the next IUI, what I had to reschedule to make it to my appointments, whether drinking water on my way to each blood draw helped my veins be more cooperative, but I do remember that it was Dr. Bonderant's father who did the actual IUI procedure. Certainly, he was older, as I had requested. Unfortunately, he was not more successful.

CHAPTER 10

▼

PARTY SEASON

Despite the depressing outcome of my unsuccessful Thanksgiving attempt at pregnancy, the holiday season continued at full speed with invitations to several Christmas parties from my office and from Steven's. We had a good feeling of settling into our new communities.

The party for the staff at my office promised to be the most fun. Everyone had voted to have the party at the rowdy steakhouse where it had been the year before, not the stuffy country club where it had been the year before that. Christmas party stories were among the favorite office lore. Two years ago, one of the doctors had invited everyone to one of the very old Atlanta country clubs, but everyone felt too constrained; they did not want waiters snapping open starched linen napkins and gracefully placing them on their laps and then having to speak quietly and politely, while sipping small sips of wine from fragile glasses. No, they wanted to go back to Longhorn's, where everyone had gotten rip-roaring drunk on Jack Daniels and had a smashing good time. Gourmet and elegant would have been my preference, but the doctors were delighted since Longhorn's cost several hundred dollars less.

The levity started the moment we hit the Hollywood Western-style doorway, with everyone trying to cram in at the same time. Last year's tales included dancing on tables and lampshades on heads. I hoped that our senior partner, who was a bit stout, was not going to test out the table tops. Frankly, I thought that if everyone was going to carry on in the manner planned, we should have chosen an establishment farther from the office, since I suspected that there was a good chance that someone would recognize at least one of the twenty of us. Our crowd had not even finished shoving through the doorway before we were recognized.

After our boisterous entrance, the hostess, a woman short for her weight, with curly red hair framing a friendly and freckly face, in a dungaree skirt a bit too short for her stocky thighs, emerged from behind her podium and hugged Alice, one of the nurses. "You were so great when I had my miscarriage," she announced, flinging her arms around Alice. "I don't know what I would have done without you." Her name tag said "PEGGY" in bold, black letters.

Alice hugged her back. "I'm glad to see you looking so well," Alice answered.

"We're trying again," Peggy continued, unconcerned about the crowd around her. "We've put together as many tables as we could to fit you all together. Please follow me."

We fell into line and obediently followed Peggy around large, wooden round tables full of jovial conversations, to a wall of long rectangular tables, somewhat out of the way. The first people in line slid in, and, like eager kindergartners, shimmied to the far end of the bench. Soon the two rows of seats were filled, and the hostess was handing out menus. "Just start us out with some pitchers of sangria," Dr. Halle called to no one in particular.

Within moments, the bright red sangria was flowing. I felt as if I were back in high school. Definitely, left out of the cool crowd. No drinking during fertility attempts. I was never quite sure why women can not drink when they are trying to get pregnant. It was clear to me that men were told to stay away from alcohol up to 72 days before conception because they are forever growing new sperm, which may be adversely effected by events or consumptions of the moment, but women have their eggs for life. In fact, a baby girl fetus at about twenty weeks has the most eggs that her ovaries will ever have. Well before birth, my biological clock had started ticking. Now, even a pitcher of sangria, with its bright red liquid accented by cheerful, juicy orange slices, sent me spinning into a private fertility pity party.

Sensing someone behind me, I twisted in my chair to see a young woman holding a baby. "Sorry, to bother you while you're out, but I just had to say hello," she said, clearly to me. She looked vaguely familiar, with dyed blond hair, roots turning brown, rosy red cheeks and a bright smile with perfectly straight teeth. Her matching green silk slacks and blouse both had stains from her lunch.

"Not at all," I answered, genuinely delighted that someone would seek me out. I turned in my seat as much as the crowded table allowed.

"I just wanted to show you my baby," she continued. "I'm having lunch with some girl friends. I think your group delivered all of their babies. They were too shy to come over. But, I just wanted to thank you for my baby. You were such a hero. And, I love him so much." There were tears in her eyes.

"That was quite a night," I said, still not sure who she was. "I am glad everything turned out so well. What a beautiful baby," I added.

Weeks of not sleeping and nursing every three hours had obviously taken their toll, but she was as put together as a new mother could be. Her clothing matched and was attractively tailored, even if it was a bit too bright in the green department. Her hair appeared to have been recently styled and brushed into place before leaving the house, although she needed to have the color touched up, and the make-up could not hide the bags under her eyes. It was impossible to eat while holding a baby who was still too small for a high chair without spilling on yourself. Despite the food stains and dark circles under her eyes, she looked radiant, and I envied her.

She kneeled next to my chair to give me a better view of the baby asleep on her shoulder. As I stroked her sleeping baby's cheek, she asked me, "Don't you want children?"

Well, now there was the question of the hour. How should I answer? In fact, people asked me that *all* the time. I should have a pat answer. Every time someone asked me, however, I toyed with the idea of spilling my guts, of bursting into tears and telling them, that yes, I desperately wanted children, that I wished that I had gotten pregnant in high school or college, when I might have still been fertile, and that I was terribly jealous of their easy fertility.

"Maybe one day," I answered, with a forced smile.

"I just love Jonathan," she continued. "You can not imagine it until you have your own. It is the most amazing love. It's not like anything I've ever felt before. It's just amazing and wonderful." The baby was drooling onto her silk blouse, forming a dark black spot spreading out from under his mouth, blissfully asleep.

It had taken me a while to place her face, but when she said "Jonathan," I remembered the night of her delivery. She had called around 3:30 a.m. to tell me that her water had broken. As she answered my other questions, I learned that it was her first baby, that she had not been dilated on her last visit to the office two days before, and that she was not having any contractions. The baby kicked actively, as usual. All of that meant that it might be more than 36 hours until she had her baby. Some doctors would have told her to wait at home for contractions to start, or for twelve hours from her water breaking, whichever came first. I told her that she probably had time to take a shower, but, since her water had broken, she should come in to the hospital sooner rather than later. I advised her that if the baby's movements decreased or stopped she should come in right away. She apologized for waking me, and I assured her that I was already wide awake at the hospital with another patient.

After I hung up the phone in the call room, I called labor and delivery to check on another patient who was in labor. A nurse told me that the patient was contracting in a good pattern, that the baby looked good, and that the patient had been comfortably asleep since getting her epidural one hour earlier. I lay back down in the call room, for about another two hours, tossing and turning, wondering if I should check my laboring patient, or let us both sleep. Two hours later, I got up to check her. She was completely dilated, and well rested. She was ready to start pushing. As the nurse was getting her ready to push, I hurried to take my shower, knowing that the delivery could easily come anytime during my morning ritual of taking a shower, having breakfast in the cafeteria and rounding on the post partum patients. After a long night, a shower and brushing your teeth are crucial to starting off a new day.

I was just settling in to enjoy the hot water cascading down my back when my pager beeped. I stepped out of the shower to check it: 7700–911! Thank goodness I had not gotten to the shampoo, yet. What could have become an emergency in the last seven minutes? I hastily rubbed myself once with the tiny, harsh hospital towel, threw on my underwear, scrubs and clogs and ran down the short hallway to Labor and Delivery.

"Heart tones down in Room 6," called the charge nurse from the nursing station.

"But, my patient is in Room 8," I answered, immediately planning to be annoyed that I had been pulled out of the shower for another doctor's patient, while that doctor was at home, possibly still asleep.

"Just got here," she answered.

"Please have someone bring in the ultrasound machine," I asked, as I pushed open the door to Room 6. There was a general air of panic in the room. I walked over to the patient and introduced myself. I had not yet met her in the office. She looked about 25 years old, with radiant, clear skin, deep blue eyes and light brown hair. Sitting propped up in the bed in her hospital gown, her uterus seemed about to swallow her entire being. As I asked her a few preliminary questions and established that she was the woman from the phone call with a totally simple, uncomplicated pregnancy. I looked at the fetal heart rate tracing. After her arrival about fifteen minutes ago, she had been placed on the fetal heart rate monitor and had about ten minutes of a beautiful heart rate tracing, meeting all the criteria to reassure us that the baby was fine, a baseline between 120 and 160 beats per minute, with what are called accelerations, a speeding up of the heart rate for a few seconds, then returning to baseline. Then, four minutes ago, the heart rate had plummeted to the 60's.

The nurses had already put an oxygen mask over her face and tried changing her position.

"What's mom's heart rate?" I asked, as I pulled on sterile gloves and moved around the bed to check her cervix, trying to ascertain if we had a true emergency, with a baby in jeopardy, or merely a technical error. Maybe the baby's head was rapidly coming down and the monitor was now picking up the mother's heart rate, which should be between 60 and 80. Maybe the baby had descended rapidly and would be delivered in two pushes. The latter was unlikely, since she appeared to be in no pain, but checking her cervix would provide some answers and, possibly, some reassurance. While manually checking her cervix, I could put a monitor on the baby's head, to be sure that the heart rate we were looking at was the baby's and not the mother's.

"Eighty," answered the nurse.

Not a good sign; the maternal heart rate was higher than baby's. Her cervix was still closed, so I could not put a monitor on the baby's scalp.

Still hoping for a technical error to explain the alarmingly low heart rate, I squirted gel on her belly and looked with the ultrasound. Yes, the baby's heart rate was only sixty, less than half of what it should be!

"Call anesthesia, tell them we're going back," I told the nurse. I did not have to tell her this was a dire emergency and we had to act quickly.

As I unplugged the electric bed from the wall and began moving the bed toward the door, I explained to this bewildered couple, neither of whom I had ever seen, "Your baby's heart tones are very low. I don't know why, but it is a sign that the baby is in trouble. We need to do a C-Section, right now." Glancing at the monitor to read her name, I reassured her, "Sonya, you're going to be fine. We'll take good care of you."

"Just save my baby. Save my little Jonathan," she said from behind her uterus. "Do whatever you have to do," Sonya instructed, with a voice at once full of confidence and fear.

"We'll send someone out to let you know what's happening," I called to the husband, as I headed out the door, pulling the bed behind me. Real emergencies are one of the few times that husbands can't be in the delivery room. Sonya would have to be put to sleep with general anesthesia, and no one could take time to deal with the father in the operating room.

I wheeled the bed down the hall. A nurse took the bed from me as I entered the operating suite, and stopped to put on my cap, mask and booties. After coaching Sonya how to maneuver her very pregnant belly and hips from the bed to the operating table, I stepped into the hallway to scrub while the nurse rechecked the heart tones. "They're in the fifties," she called.

I scrubbed quickly and the anesthesiologist, Dr. Dutch, a wonderful man in his late 40's with slightly graying hair and a former athlete's body, ran behind me into the room. As I dried my hands and pulled on my sterile surgical gown and gloves, Dr. Dutch started Sonya's intravenous line, and explained to her that she would be awake until the last moment, that she would feel me clean her off. I poured betadyne from a bowl onto her belly, lay down the drapes and said, "Ready," with false calmness in my voice.

"Go!" said Dr. Dutch, as soon as Sonya was asleep.

I cut quickly and firmly, piercing the skin and fat in one layer. With the next layer, I cut through the fascia, then tented the firm white tissue, and cut it away from the muscles underneath. I put my finger through the soft, filmy peritoneum, put in the bladder protector, cut one more layer, separating the bladder from the uterus, and the cut into the uterus. I entered the cavity where the baby was with my fingers. The umbilical cord popped out, indicating that it had been compressed against the wall of the uterus. The baby's cord was wrapped around his neck three times. Either one of these might have explained the fetal distress. After pressing the cord back into the uterus, delivering the baby's head and suctioning out the mouth, I unwrapped the cord from around the baby's neck, clamped the cord and handed the limp baby to the neonatal team. "Please be okay," I prayed.

The baby stayed in the neonatal intensive care unit overnight, but was in his mother's arms, nursing, when I came by to make rounds the next day.

How odd to remember those moments of intense fear and anxiety while sitting at Longhorn's watching everyone around me drink sangria. "Enjoy little Jonathan," I said, as Sonya stood up and went back to join her friends.

Our table got louder and louder. The sangria flowed. A few people ordered stronger drinks. Finally, the food came and a hush fell over the table as everyone focused on using their huge knives to cut into their steaks.

After dessert, it was clear that a few people had succeeded in getting too drunk to drive home. Since most of the office staff lived nearby, those who could drive drove those who could not. Anyone who needed to could pick up their car the next day.

The next party was on a Saturday night at Dr. Halle's house. "Wow," I blurted out as Steven and I approached the glow of white lights against the black winter sky. "It looks like the White House." We pulled up behind a long row of cars in the street the equivalent of a city block to the pillars at the end of the long driveway. Clearly, I had chosen the wrong shoes. My feet hurt before we were half way to the house.

Mrs. Halle had done a magnificent job decorating the house for Christmas. The house had been on the "Tour of Homes" that fall, so everything was in tip top shape. A pine wreath with green and red plaid cloth braided into it on the door led into a warm, but elegant very open interior dominated by a 14 foot Christmas tree decorated all in white with a gold star at the top. The living room merged into the kitchen, creating a more spacious feel than either amply large room would have alone. We started at the bar, a shiny, marble top with mirrors and a sink, built into the living room. I asked for a Perrier, and Steven got an O'Doule's non-alcoholic beer. Dr. Halle greeted me graciously and introduced Steven and me into the conversation. He and a neighbor were talking about their last trip to Las Vegas and exchanging gambling stories. I had once won twenty-five dollars from a quarter slot machine, but this was clearly a different league. Listening, I realized the gambling world had an entire language and culture that I knew almost nothing about. That was fine with me. I could only imagine how much money you had to spend/lose to be "comped" a free hotel room at the nicer casinos. As the conversation turned to sports, I decided it would be a polite time to compliment Mrs. Halle on her beautiful home and to join the women in the kitchen discussing their children and their decorating plans.

When we were back in the privacy of our own car heading home, Steven made the only complaint about his sacrifices in the whole fertility process. "Boy, I could sure have used a stiff drink at that party."

CHAPTER 11

▼

EVERY MORNING

Starting the IVF cycle earned us a trip back to Dr. Bonderant's office to meet with him personally, not just his nurse. He discussed what would be involved, starting with that day, when Steven would practice giving me injections by sticking a needle into an orange. The wrist action of thrusting the needle was very important. Dr. Bonderant and Elizabeth both emphasized this strategy, as if they were explaining how to lob a tennis ball into the far court, instead of a needle into my behind. They were an impressive pair, and you would trust them on strategy, Dr. Bondurant in his neatly pressed white coat, his designer pants showing underneath, and Elizabeth in her pressed aqua scrub suit, with her many braids neatly in a bun and her make-up just the right tones for her face.

Was my skin really that tough? There was an inflammatory breast cancer in which the skin condition is called "Peau d'orange" or orange skin. Not a pretty image. At least Steven had never seen it. Breast cancer brought my thoughts back to Stacey; I was already three years older than she had been when she died. My treatments would be nothing compared to chemotherapy. I asked myself if I would be willing to give up my life to have a child and, then, why any woman should have to make that decision. Why did our bodies not cooperate?

Dr. Bonderant was still talking about what would happen today. We would move from visceral issues of fruit and the body to more cut and dry issues of the wallet. After the orange lesson, we would meet with the financial officer, which might be much more painful.

The first step, Dr. Bonderant explained, as if this explanation was just for me and he had not already given this talk five times that day, and hundreds or thousands of times before that, was to shut down my cycle with Lupron, an anti-estrogen. "Amy," he continued, personalizing his routine by adding my name, "this will involve daily injections, but just subcutaneous, right under the skin." He did not mention that these injections were nothing compared to what came next.

What came next were daily intramuscular injections of hormones to stimulate my ovaries, followed by another intramuscular injection of beta-HCG to make me ovulate when my estrogen was high enough and my follicles (eggs in my ovaries) were big enough. Even those shots would not hurt nearly as much as the next step; progesterone in oil, which required a super-size needle because the oil was so thick. This was the part where the wrist action that Steven practiced with the orange was the most important.

Another cycle of IUI, or even just trying on our own for a while, was sounding better and better, but I knew that would just be a waste of time, and my biological clock was ticking away, tick tock. I remembered how depressed I had been after a lecture in residency when they told us that fertility actually declined at 30, not 35. Why didn't anyone mention that on your first day of medical school? Why had I taken time off between college and medical school to enjoy life and live a little? It was too late, now. The super-size needle would be my penance for two years spent away from the grindstone, going to clubs that didn't open until midnight, hanging out with neighbors, seeing all the latest movies on opening night, and never missing an aerobics class.

Dr. Bonderant pushed a button and Elizabeth appeared to lead us in to yet another section of the fertility clinic. Although it was equally well-appointed, it seemed harsher. Steven sat in the assigned chair and was given an orange and a syringe. The nurse instructed him to pinch the sides of the orange to make a bump before stabbing it with the needle. She explained the importance of the wrist motion, that it was a thrusting or stabbing motion. Being gentle and slow would just prolong the agony. Steven earnestly stabbed the orange, flicking his wrist like the end of a tennis serve, and depressed the plunger on the syringe. He repeated the maneuvers until Elizabeth approved of his technique. "Well done," she said, sounding like a BBC sports announcer.

After she explained how to measure and draw up the medication, she told me the really bad news: I would have to come in every single day for several weeks to have blood drawn and ultrasound monitoring.

"How early can I make the appointments?" I asked in horror, imagining explaining to my partners that I would have to cancel my first five or ten patients of the day for several weeks.

"If you don't come for the tests, we will cancel your cycle," Elizabeth said with British boarding school firmness, perhaps even a bit harshly.

I didn't say I wasn't coming, I thought, defensively. "I'll be here," I assured her.

"Good," she said. "The first ultrasound appointments are at 7:30. They usually don't take more than fifteen minutes, unless you're lucky enough to have a lot of follicles to count."

She handed us a thick packet of papers and instructed us to fill them out before we returned for our next visit. If the consents were not signed, the cycle would be canceled.

Then, she led us to the financial officer, a woman in a tight blue suit, the skirt of which seemed to pin her legs together. Her unyielding brown eyes and pointy face left no room for negotiation. Although I explained that it was my impression that my insurance would cover one IVF cycle, she insisted that we sign a large stack of forms confirming our personal financial obligation. An IVF cycle cost about $12,000. That included the ultrasounds, the blood tests, the egg retrieval, processing of the sperm, the laboratory process for growing the embryo(s) and implantation. If we needed ICSI (intracytoplamic sperm injection), if the sperm did not enter the egg on its own and had to be injected in, that would cost extra. I was pretty sure Steven's guys could make it, but maybe my eggs would just be too tough. That was not decided until the sperm were run past the eggs, and I don't recall the exact price for it, but it was extra.

The price also did not include medications. Conveniently, these could be bought at the pharmacy in the building. How much could medicines cost? I thought.

Fine. I asked if we needed to sign anything now. Yes, on the last page of the large stack of papers, there was a line for our signatures, promising that we would pay. They did not seem interested in my first born as collateral. I guess, given the nature of their business, that would have been a big risk. Where would Rumplestiltskin be if that princess had been infertile? I signed without reading.

On the way to the check out desk, I perused my bill and noticed that there was a charge for the financial consultation!

The next shock was at the pharmacy. The pharmacy was on the first floor of the parking deck, tucked into a corner and very compact. There were three neat rows of products, but nothing superfluous like hairspray or nail polish. This tiny place was devoted to the fertility business, with no room for bright, bouncy beach balls or reclining lawn chairs. The balding pharmacist had an ingratiating smile and was very friendly and accommodating, reviewing the basics of giving an injection, and, again, emphasizing the importance of the wrist action. He told us that he was throwing in the box of alcohol swabs for free. He made sure that we had all of the syringes and needles that we would need, as well as the requisite plastic, red biohazard box in which to dispose of all of this medical waste. The pharmacist arranged everything in several bags, put them on the counter and then, nonchallantly handed Steven the bill, with a motion similar to a handshake. $1200! At least the alcohol wipes were free.

On the appointed day after my period, which, of course, came early in the morning on the appointed day, not allowing me even a moment to hope that I might be pregnant, I started giving myself the subcutaneous Lupron injections. That night, out to dinner with one of my doctor girl friends, Samantha, I excused myself to go to the ladies' room. Now, I had joined the ranks of the Cool People. After locking the stall, I sat down on the seat, opened my purse, drew up my medicine and "shot up" in the bathroom. Of course, your average junkie may not be quite as meticulous about sterile technique, cleaning with an alcohol swab first and dropping the used needle and syringe into a handy, purse-sized red, plastic biohazard box. The Lupron was probably as expensive as any fix.

While using Lupron, Steven and I were again subjected to the indignity of using condoms while trying to get pregnant. I had many patients who claimed that they had gotten pregnant with condoms. Not me; I just got antisperm antibodies.

Every night, I carefully read my instruction sheet, since each day had a different set of procedures. Even for a doctor, it was confusing.

In the morning before the first intramuscular shot, Steven seemed a bit nervous. Shannon, one of the nurses from my office, kindly volunteered to come to our house and either watch him do it or to do it herself. She even volunteered to come every night while I needed injections. I could tell that Steven was tempted, but, after much discussion, we decided that Steven would give the shots, under professional guidance, until he got it right. The first night, Shannon watched him do it, and I pretended that it did not hurt. Shannon told me that if you rub the area after you give a shot, it not only helped to absorb the medicine, but helped to decrease the pain. That was a nursing school tip; they did not teach any tricks for giving shots in medical school, since that was a nursing skill. That pain, the pain of getting a big, huge needle in your buttock, was referred to by physicians, like me, as "discomfort."

Although, I rearranged my schedule so that I was not totally stressed out about getting to the office on time, I was still often the first patient to arrive at the fertility clinic to have my blood drawn. Then, I joined the other professional women in tailored suits with well-coiffed hair, checking their watches every few minutes, in the waiting room. We all had meetings, appointments, clients or patients waiting for us.

The pressure and unfairness of it all was getting to me; we had all "done the right thing." We were all contributing members of society, having worked not just hard, but very hard, at every step of the way.

On one of those days, after returning from the fertility clinic to my own office, I saw Mandi, a baby-faced chubby 16 year old with locks of blond hair, who could have been an angel in a Christmas pageant, except for her 36 week pregnant belly. She was with her 20-something year old boyfriend. Neither of them seemed to have any place to be. Neither of them worked or went to school. I asked her, "What do you do all day, just have sex?"

She rolled her eyes at me, in that surly teenage way, but her boyfriend at least had the decency to cast his eyes toward the floor in embarrassment.

Later that day, I spent a long time counseling Leanne, a tall, thin, actually scrawny, 40 year old woman with skin and teeth that told of a hard life, but whose green eyes still sparkled despite her hardships. She had missed a few periods. Since she had not slept with her husband in over a year, she was hoping that she was in menopause. In fact, her urine pregnancy test was positive, and the ultrasound showed that she was twelve weeks pregnant.

"What should I tell my children?" Leanne asked me, with more than a hint of desperation in her voice. "They're teenagers. It's so hard to get them to do the right thing, and we're a religious family."

"What were you using for birth control?" I asked, not yet having an answer of what to tell her children.

"My husband had a vasectomy," she answered.

Staring at her from across my desk, I refrained from reminding her that she had not been sleeping with her husband and that vasectomies were non-transferable. Her husband's vasectomy had failed to protect her from the flattery and kind attention from her manager at K-Mart.

She reiterated that, since they were a religious family, she would definitely keep the baby, but what should she tell her children? I referred her back to her church for guidance in that matter, and emphasized the importance of prenatal vitamins.

And then, there were those of us pacing at the fertility clinic. I had heard that a lot of people made friends in the waiting room. Two days in a row, I sat next to a sturdy-looking, blond woman who did not look a bit infertile to me. Each day she wore a different, very expensive, nicely tailored suit. This was her third cycle. The first cycle had been canceled because her ovaries did not grow follicles large enough. For the next cycle, she had been on what she described as "massive" doses of medicine, which had made her quite crazy and caused nightmares. She gave a nervous giggle, which contrasted with her professional banker attire, as she described how her ever-supportive husband claimed not to have noticed, or not to have minded, her wild mood swings. She said that he did not really care if they had children or not. He was "fine" if it worked or not.

That was the scariest part, the part that I tried not to think about: the husband. Many marriages had fallen apart under less stress. Did Steven care if I could not get pregnant? Clearly, he had wonderful sperm. That was all that he needed to have children. Would he just leave me and find someone else? Why wouldn't he? Why shouldn't he? Children seemed so central to life, to being a family, to living on after you died. He could easily find some fertile woman who would marry him in an instant. These fears rushed through my mind in the one second of this woman's giggle. Did she really have a husband who did not care about having children, but was willing to spend tens of thousands of dollars in pursuit of them? Did he love her more than the future he had always imagined for himself, sitting at the dinner table, children telling about their day at school?

I listened as she explained that the second time, she had grown only two eggs, had gone through the entire in vitro process, but then not gotten pregnant. Her eggs did not seem to be growing well this time, either.

She earnestly wished me luck, as she was called for her ultrasound. Walking across the bright, spacious waiting room to the tiny, dark ultrasound room where, with your legs up in stirrups you saw in black and white your first hint of success or failure measured in little black circles, I decided that I could not become her friend: if I got pregnant and she did not, I would feel too guilty, and I did not want my mind playing more games with my ovaries than it already did. In addition, I really did not like looking my fears in the face like that. Successful career woman fails at reproduction.

In the morning, I barely had time for my blood work and ultrasounds. At the end of the day, I had to scramble to make sure that I received the nurse's call about my blood work. With those results came my individual instructions for the evening. From my dramatic, almost tearful, in fact, nearly hysterical, reaction to my brief encounter with this other patient, it looked as if I would have to make time for RESOLVE, the support group for fertility patients. When on earth was I going to do that? Certainly, I was not going to ask my partners to cover for me while I went to group therapy for women who failed to get pregnant and could not handle it. I was supposed to be the "tough but sensitive" new woman of the future. The sensitive was not supposed to overshadow the tough.

The technologist, in her starched white coat, emerged with my new friend, with whom I did not want to become friends. Either she had only been in there a few minutes or I had gotten lost in my thoughts, and it really had been a while. My friend emerged behind her, a stoic smile showing perfectly straight, white teeth, outlined neatly with subtle make-up which looked as professional as a newscaster's. "Maybe next time," she said to me, as she tightened her grip on her shiny, burgundy briefcase. "If it doesn't work next time, I may try to convince Ned to let me adopt." Her ultrasound had only lasted a few minutes. There had been no eggs to count or to measure.

No proper etiquette exists for the transition from supporting a friend with a heart wrenching life decision to time for your own ultrasound. "I hope it all works out for you," I answered, standing as my name was called. I hoped that Ned loved her as much as she thought. I hoped that Ned really did not care if they had children, but would spend another ten thousand dollars for another cycle and then another ten thousand dollars for the cost of an adoption. If he really did not care about having children, the adoption would be a harder sell. Steven and I had not even talked about adoption. He probably had never even thought that this might not work, that I might fail. Neither of us had ever failed at anything. How could we fail now, when it really mattered.

I braced myself as I walked toward the ultrasound room. What if my eggs weren't growing well? What if none grew? What if I emerged from the ultrasound room in less than five minutes and everyone waiting, in a hurry to get to work, knew that I, too, had failed. What if I had so many eggs that it took so long to count and measure them that I was late for work?

"Good morning, Amy," the technologist greeted me, cheerfully. How could she be so cheerful? I was still depressed about my friend, whose name I had already forgotten, not having enough eggs for her cycle for the third time in a row.

"How many cycles will they let her do," I asked, from personal, as well as professional, interest.

"Who?" the technologist asked.

"I don't know her name," I answered. "The woman you just scanned. This was her third failed cycle."

"I don't know much about what goes on outside this room, but I rarely see people back more than two or three cycles if things aren't working out." She held up a sheet and I obediently undressed behind it, then sat on the table, laid back and put my feet in the stirrups.

"Don't forget about my latex allergy," I said, as she slipped a latex glove onto the ultrasound probe.

"Oh, right," she said. "Wait just a moment." Stepping out of the room, she left me to my thoughts and worries. How many follicles would I have? How big would they be? How long would it take to measure them? Would I make it to the office in time? Was it worth mentioning my latex allergy, because she still was not back yet, and I would have patients waiting for me in my office in a few minutes, and that was on the other side of town. If traffic was bad this morning, I would be late. I should have brought my own latex-free gloves. How could I not have brought my own gloves? I should have known this would happen. I was wasting precious time, and I could have prevented this. If my nameless friend had had a successful cycle, I would have been even later. How could I even have such thoughts? Of course, I would not mind being late if she could get pregnant and have her own children. I would gladly be late so that she could have lots of big, juicy follicles. But, I should not be late on my own account. Sure, I could. These were my babies. My patients could just wait. When I got to the office, I would ask the secretary to cancel my patients until ten o'clock tomorrow morning. But, what if I did not need to, what if I did not have any follicles? Just the thought of ovaries with no follicles brought tears to my eyes and I could feel them welling up in the corners of my eyes by the time the technologist came back in with a hand-ful of non-latex gloves.

"I brought some extras for tomorrow," she said. I flinched as she said that, afraid that planning for the best would cause the worst.

Fortunately, my eggs were growing beautifully. Each day, they got just the right amount bigger. Each afternoon, a nurse called me and told me how much medicine to inject that night. If I could not get to the phone, she left a message with one of nurses in my office. That was handy, but meant that absolutely every-body knew all of my business. Everyone claimed to be excited about my follicles' growth. I hoped that it did not put too much pressure on the poor little guys.

One call day, I had 21 eggs and my ovaries measured 14 centimeters each. Fortunately, I felt fine, totally normal, in fact. Still, I tried to walk very smoothly, to glide along the ground, so as not to disturb them. When ovaries got that big, they could torse, or twist. Ovarian torsion is a medical emergency requiring immediate surgery to prevent the ovary from becoming strangled. You could lose your entire ovary if it twists. Then, you lost another six weeks of work recovering from the surgery. I did not have time for that kind of complication.

Being on call meant that I had to make numerous trips from the office to the hospital to check on patients who were in labor. I told the Labor and Delivery nurses that I was moving slowly that day and asked them to give me a few extra minutes to get to any deliveries. As I walked across the covered walk-way to the hospital, I kept picturing the image from the ultrasound machine, huge ovaries swollen with lots of eggs.

When the nurse from the fertility clinic called that afternoon, I was at the hospital, in the middle of a delivery. She left a message that it was time for the beta-HCG injection. The beta-HCG was only given one night of the cycle and, of course, I had not brought that particular vial with me. There were too many patients for me to drive home to pick it up. It was not the type of medicine the hospital pharmacy stocked, and it cost a fortune. Ever my knight in shining armor, Steven volunteered to bring the medicine to the hospital.

We actually had time not just for him to give me the shot, but to have dinner between deliveries. I scarfed down my food a little less wolfishly than I had as a resident, but I had to answer my pager five times before I finished my meal. My manners were ruined for life.

With the beta-HCG on Thursday, the egg retrieval would be on a Saturday. Great! I would not have to cancel any patients. The egg retrieval was done at the fertility clinic, with intravenous anesthesia. You could not just do it first thing in the morning and then jump up and drive to the office. Because you had to fast overnight for the anesthesia, they were done first thing in the morning. Now, the first thing in the morning turned out to be a bad thing, because I could not work a full day and then stop by to be put to sleep and harvested at the end of the day. Saturday would be perfect.

I had seen some egg retrievals in residency, but I was blissfully asleep for my own. A long needle was introduced into my vagina and, with ultrasound guidance, the eggs were sucked up into a syringe. I saw the doctor who was going to do it for a few seconds, before the anesthesiologist sent me to sleep.

Successfully growing 21 eggs does not guarantee that any of them will work. Steven and I waited anxiously for several days until we got the call that several embryos had grown, and were ready to be implanted the next afternoon.

Steven arranged to be there and we arrived in the lobby at the same time, holding hands in the elevator. We did not wait in the waiting room, but were taken down a hallway which looked very scientific. Although I could not actually see the laboratory on the other side of the wall, I imagined a sterile, white room, brimming with microscopes, test tubes and petri dishes, with scientists in white coats scurrying about.

A very business-like nurse in pressed aqua scrubs introduced herself as "Alisha" and showed us into a room. After dutifully trading my bottom garments for the sheet, I sat on the white paper on the exam table. A technician, looking exactly as I had expected in a starched white coat and marine-style short brown hair, came in from a side door that connected to the laboratory. He asked if we wanted to see pictures of our embryos. Of course we wanted to; these pictures might be as close to baby pictures as I would ever get. He flashed a video image from a microscope in another room onto a television screen in our room, pointing out our name, emphasizing that there had been no confusion, no mix-ups, and that we would, in fact, be getting the correct embryos.

Despite my scientific background, I was a bit shocked by how much my potential future children looked like the picture on the cover of my medical school text book called *Cell Biology*. Nonetheless, I asked the nice man in the white coat if the video made pictures, and he kindly printed a picture of our three little embryos and handed it to us. He explained that these three were the "best of the lot." There were five more that did not look as good, but still looked good enough to freeze for future use.

He left and Steven and I just looked at each other, a rare moment when we were both at a loss for words. A few minutes later, another doctor came in. I recognized his name; he was one of the founders of this tremendously successful group. He barely looked at me and said, "Put your feet up here, honey." His attention was focused on the petri dish the technician was holding. That was fine with me. These little guys you *really* did not want to drop. Dropping sperm that took five to twenty minutes to procure with the aid of pornographic magazines was one thing. Weeks of painful injections, blood draws and early-morning harried ultrasounds had gone into the creation of these little guys from *Cell Biology*.

Without another word, the famous doctor sat on a stool between my legs. I could not see much after that. Steven held my hand, as close as we could get in this act of potential procreation. I did not cramp at all. I interpreted lack of cramping as a bad sign, that nothing had actually entered my uterus. I hoped that this fancy fertility specialist had actually put the embryos in my uterus and not just dropped them into the vagina or not even squeezed them out of the syringe.

When he was finished, the doctor looked at my chart and asked, somewhat sheepishly, which one of us was the doctor.

I volunteered that I was.

"What's your specialty?" he asked, changing his tone from the little "honey" of a moment ago.

"OB/GYN," I answered, thinking, that he was not at the top of my list for referrals. With a six month waiting list and people flying in from all over world to see him, he probably did not care.

He said that I should lie there for twenty minutes, that I could prop a pillow under my bottom, but that it probably would not make any difference, and then I could go home. After he left the room, Alisha told me to come back in ten days for a blood test to see if I was pregnant. I stayed for thirty minutes and then went home to lie in bed, hoping to trick at least one of these embryos into thinking that I was indeed a desirable body in which to implant.

CHAPTER 12

▼

172 BEATS PER MINUTE

I could not possibly have waited ten days to find out if I was pregnant. Not only was I dying to find out if I was finally pregnant, I still had to get those nasty progesterone in oil injections every day. I did some reading to find out what the first possible day was that I might have a positive pregnancy test. I waited past that day and the next. The following day, I asked Shannon, who had followed my trials with me daily, to draw some blood from me. I walked to the hospital and personally handed the precious vial of my blood to Dr. Scott, the chairman of the pathology department. Dr. Scott was a friendly man, with hair just beginning to turn a bit silver, who always took time to go over my patients slides' with me when I came to the lab to look at them. In the midst of our friendly chat, I mentioned that the sample was my blood and that I had just finished an IVF cycle; he kindly volunteered to run it himself, right away.

I waited. And waited. It was only several minutes, but I heard each second tick on the clock over my head. Finally, he handed me a slip of shiny white paper generated by the machine that had read my blood sample: 365. "That's high," he noted, smiling. "Might be more than one."

I hardly dared to hope for one. I wanted to hug him, except that he was behind one of those sliding glass, lab windows. I was alone, in a white waiting room, full of empty chairs, sharing one of the happiest moments of my life with a man behind a glass window. But, wait, I was not alone. At least one of my friends from *Cell Biology* had decided to stay! I walked very gently back to the office, partly because I was walking on air, and partly to provide a smooth ride for my new rider, or riders.

I decided not to tell anyone in the office, but my big smile gave me away the moment I walked in the door. One of the nurses asked, "Any news?"

I just smiled, trying to hold back tears that I felt welling up in the corners of my eyes.

She gave me a big hug.

"It might not work, though," I said, quickly. "It might just be a chemical pregnancy." About 25% of all conceptions don't make it, especially when you know from such an early point. I often felt that many of my patients would have been better off not doing a pregnancy test when they were 12 hours late for their period. If you don't know you're pregnant that early, you just think that you are a few days late and having a heavy period, rather than going through the anguish of a miscarriage. After everything that I had been through, though, I would be in anguish if I was not pregnant.

As my little secret blazed through the office, I tucked my treasured piece of paper with the precious number 365 on it into the pocket of my white coat, picked up a chart from a door and went into an exam room. I no longer resented my pregnant teenagers, although I still felt that they would be best served to have finished high school. I also wondered how we had so many pregnant patients from the local jail. They were always pleasant and surprisingly cheerful in their orange jump suits. A doctor's visit was probably a nice change from whatever the daily routine involved. I always tried to figure out how they had gotten pregnant in jail. It was hard to get a straight answer to "How long have you been in jail?" since most were in and out. All of them were in for violation of probation; no one seemed to have committed an actual crime. The closest that I could find to a reason for incarceration or probation was a woman who told me that she was arrested for failure to pay alimony or child support. That struck me as grossly unfair, given all the dead beat dads out there.

I had entered a new club, the club of women with positive pregnancy tests. Me, who could barely get an ovulation kit to turn blue or pink or whatever shade the kit claimed should happen, had finally gotten a positive pregnancy test. It was a goal unto itself. I had done it! I had always been a believer in hard work, and hard work had paid off. Of course, I wouldn't have minded not having to work quite so hard, but now it had worked. I was pregnant! I had a number on a piece of paper to prove it.

I smiled my way through the afternoon, a kind, empathic physician. My nurse nudged me along; I was being too kind, spending too much time with each patient and getting behind. The patients in the waiting room were getting upset about the wait.

Steven was happy, but, like me, remained cautious. I was not certain that he understood my sense of accomplishment from just getting pregnant, just getting those few, microscopic cells to stick to me long enough to release some pregnancy hormones. I had taken tests all of my life, taken them seriously, and usually done well. Whenever Steven and I moved to a new state, we always quizzed each other on our way to the new Department of Motor Vehicles to make sure that we aced our written driving tests. We rehearsed how many feet to park from a fire hydrant, how many feet to stop behind a school bus. We knew it all. Not to mention all the tests from kindergarten on, on which we had scored well above our grade level and gotten ourselves in and through Yale and graduate schools. And now, finally, I had passed my pregnancy test.

For the first time since this process began, I was no longer resentful of all of those years of successful contraception when I had never had to decide between my career and a child, carry a secret pregnancy or terminate an unwanted pregnancy. That day, I felt lucky, "blessed" as I've learned to say since moving to the South. Shannon would no longer pat my hand and say, "Bless your heart," after some fertility set back.

Two days later, I rechecked my blood level. This time it was done officially, at the fertility clinic. Dr. Bonderant himself called to congratulate me. Not only was my pregnancy level excellent, my progesterone level also looked good.

"Do I have to keep getting those painful shots?" I asked, hopefully. I knew there were other methods of keeping progesterone levels high; intravaginal cream, messy and expensive, but painless, and tablets, also painless and not so expensive.

"With IVF, we want to keep all of our bases covered. The shots are the best," he answered.

"Steven's gotten pretty good at it," I laughed. "It would be a shame to waste that talent."

"Keep up the good work," Dr. Bonderant said, before giving me instructions on when to return for more blood tests and ultrasounds.

As with the pregnancy test, I couldn't quite wait until the ultrasound Dr. Bonderant ordered. I would have been happy to wait, since I did not want anything to burst my bubble. I was actually terrified of the ultrasound. I didn't want to know if I just had a chemical pregnancy or if it wasn't growing well. Nonetheless, my friend Samantha, with more confidence in me than I had in myself, convinced me to come to her office to do an ultrasound at the first possible date that we might have seen something.

Steven left work early that day and came with me. As I sat in Samantha's waiting room, I wished that I had not come. We should just have gone out for dinner. Holding Steven's hand, I told him that I wanted to leave. The other patients sitting in front of the flowered wall paper and reading glossy magazines in comfortable arm chairs all seemed to be staring at me, looking at my uterus.

"Please, don't let it be an empty sac," I thought, over and over. I looked down at my skirt, where my uterus would be. "Don't be empty," I begged, silently.

Finally, all of the patients had gone and Samantha appeared at the doorway where the nurse had been calling patients for their appointments. "Amy," she greeted me, cheerfully, "Come on back."

As I followed her around a corner and past two exam rooms, she chatted about her day. "I can't believe you've never seen my office," she quipped.

Steven nudged me.

"Me, neither," I responded, trying my best to sound calm, as if I had just dropped by to see her office, purely a social visit, not the most important moment of my life. "I like the wall paper. Your waiting room looks great. Did you decorate it yourself?"

"Actually, most of it was done when I moved in. I just added a few pieces of furniture."

By now, we were in the exam room. I started to unhook my skirt. It seemed less rude than telling Samantha that I really could not wait one more second to find out what was going on inside of me.

She stepped out while I undressed. As soon as I had the sheet draped over my lap, I sent Steven out to let her know that I was ready.

When she came in, I handed her a latex-free glove to use as a cover for the ultrasound probe.

"I remembered," Samantha laughed, and pulled out her own pair of latex-free gloves.

I held my breath as the probe went into my vagina. The last thing in there had been my babies, my three sweet little embryos.

Steven and I stared at the monitor. Two sacs, two fetuses, one heart beat. Good news. Bad news. I was not quite sure. My mind raced immediately from possibility of miscarriage to the problems with twins. If one twin was not going to make it, the earlier it made that decision, the better, for the surviving twin. Sometimes, the twin just got resorbed. The body just took it back within itself. Of course, if the body expelled one twin, the other might come out with it. With twins, my chances of developing preeclampsia, gestational, or pregnancy induced, diabetes, and preterm labor were increased.

"Just one?" Steven asked.

"I only see one heart beat," Samantha answered. Turning on the Doppler, we heard a wonderful woosh, woosh. "172 beats per minute," she announced. Then, tilting the probe she continued, "but there are definitely two sacs. The second one has a fetal pole, but I don't see a heart beat."

"Come on Baby," I prayed. I felt very attached to both of my tiny, little sacs, with fetuses measuring about 4 or 5 millimeters. Not a believer in that type of thing, I, nonetheless, directed all of my positive energy to my two little sacs. I walked carefully and ate healthily and tried not to think bad thoughts. I had to be much more careful than when I had a pelvis bursting with ripe ovarian follicles. Now, I was carrying actual lives. I desperately wanted them to believe that this was a good body in which to grow.

When Samantha rescanned me a few days later, there were two heart beats!

"You willed that," Steven joked.

He was right. I had willed that.

He, on the other hand, looked like the guy in the insurance commercial, totally shocked and overwhelmed at the thought of two babies crying at the same time, two diapers to change at the same time, two Bat or Bar Mitzvahs at the same time, two college tuitions at the same time. Of immediate concern was a wedding that we were to attend that weekend. We had plans to fly to Washington, D.C. I knew that patients came to Dr. Bonderant from all over the world. Once they got pregnant, they flew back to Cincinnati, France, Saudi Arabia, or wherever. Nonetheless, there were studies indicating that flight attendants may have a higher rate of miscarriage and I had once had a patient whose water had broken at 26 weeks, just after flying from California to the East Coast. Dr. Bonderant assured me that it was safe to fly.

Before heading to work on Thursday, I packed the car for the drive to Washington. I was on call Thursday night and pretty exhausted when I started my drive on Friday afternoon. While I drove, I ate a Ben and Jerry's Peace Pop, kept the windows open and belted out Country Western songs with the radio. Babies in-utero probably do not really hear until about 26 weeks, so I felt that the damage done first by not listening to Mozart and second by listening to Country Western music would be more than made up for by the fact that I was staying awake and, therefore, alive. I managed to stay awake enough to drive for about five hours before I pulled into some motel in North Carolina. I checked in with Steven. He promised to drive back with me and recommended that I get an early start the next day since the weather report predicted snow.

The next day, my sacs and I got an early start, but, by noon, the snow was coming down hard. I pulled over and paid a garage attendant to put the chains on my tires and continued on at 20 mph, at most. I had to pull over every half an hour or so to wipe the snow from the headlights and windshield. For my little sacs, or maybe because of my little sacs, I remained amazingly calm. They will think that their mommy has gumption, I told myself. My estrogen levels were probably in the 1000's and probably did more that anything to keep me calm as darkness set in and I continued in a driving snow storm on roads I had never traveled. Certainly, any fool would recommend embarking on a solo drive in a blizzard rather than a quick plane trip!

The wedding was wonderful and no one asked what had possessed me to drive.

A few weeks later, to my delight, I began to feel a bit queasy. I kept a plastic shopping bag next to me in the car and would occasionally throw up at stop lights. By the time I got to the office, I felt fine, ready to go, after brushing my teeth.

At some point, the senior partner, Dr. Walker, began screaming at me. After the first time, one of the nurses took me aside and explained that he did that all the time, that was just how he was and to, basically, ignore it. The first time he started yelling, I assumed that one of my patients had bled to death from a post-operative complication. What other reason would he have to be so upset? Even in residency, no one screamed. If you did not know the answer to a question, you might get a look which strongly implied that your ignorance could easily kill someone, but no one screamed. My parents had not been screamers, and certainly, Steven never raised his voice. As it turned out, he was angry that I had referred a high-risk patient to one group of doctors rather than his preferred group. Another time, he was upset because I had sent a woman over 35 for a Level II ultrasound rather than scheduling her for an amniocentesis. The other doctor ended up doing the amniocentesis anyway, and Dr. Walker lost the reimbursement for the procedure. Granted, I was new to the business end of medicine, but no one had ever yelled at me like that in my life.

One Sunday, Steven and I were waiting in line for brunch at the International House of Pancakes. One of my patients recognized me, said a friendly hello and then asked if Dr. Walker was treating me any better. I just laughed, unsure how to respond, worrying that I was not a good role model for women in this suburban community, if I looked like an abused spouse at the office.

A few weeks later, my sacs were still growing well and Steven was still giving me those awful progesterone in oil shots. I had even learned to give them to myself, when required on a busy call day. One morning, I was wearing a new silk outfit, with an elastic waist. Although I was too superstitious to buy any maternity clothes, I already needed a bit more room. As I was sitting at my desk, I felt something wet. I looked down and the bottom of my silk dress was totally red, soaked in blood. My heart started to race. I lay down under my desk, to get the weight of my uterus off my cervix. I wasn't cramping; that was good. I remembered all of the women I had scanned in emergency rooms with bleeding in pregnancy. Some had been almost hemorrhaging, and the ultrasound had still shown a heart beat. Others, with almost no bleeding had had no heart beat; their babies had died inside of them with no warning. After rewinding several emergency room scenarios in my mind, I crawled out from under my desk, picked up the phone and called Dr. Leeds, one of the women doctor's in another office, just down the hall. She told me to come right over. I did not want to stand up, but there did not seem to be any other way to get there.

I tried not to cry as I scurried out the back door of my office, not caring if anyone noticed the huge red stain on the back of my dress.

Dr. Leeds and I were often on call on the same nights. That meant that we spent hours in the doctors' lounge talking and that we were there for each other to help with emergencies in the middle of the night. She knew what was at stake here and how much this meant to me. A robust, motherly looking woman with a face that radiated wisdom and concern, she had had her own fertility problems twenty years ago, before all of this technology was available. By various means, she had a houseful of children. Even today, the technology does not work for everyone. She didn't seem to be thinking about herself, but totally concerned about me, the patient.

She invited me into her office, but I told her that I really didn't want to sit in her nicely upholstered chair. For dramatic effect, I turned around and showed her my big blood stain. Duly impressed, she immediately ushered me to the ultrasound room.

I held my breath. "I don't seem to be bleeding anymore," I said hopefully, knowing that meant nothing, except that I would not make a mess bleeding on the table.

I assumed the usual position, feet up in stirrups, bottom at the foot of the table. By now, I was fully invested in my twins, my two sacs, my two heart beats. The thought that I might still have one was of little consolation, at the moment. With all that I had been through, I deserved two babies.

Dr. Leeds adjusted the ultrasound monitor so that I could watch it with her. The sacs were big enough now that only one could be seen at a time. I tried not to mutter out loud, as I prayed the hardest I have ever prayed for anything. Finally, the monitor showed one heart beat. My eyes were glued so hard to the screen that I did not even feel the probe being moved. Second heart beat. "Oh, thank God," I sighed.

"Go home and lie down," she said.

"I need to go back and let my partners know," I returned.

"I'll tell them," she said. "You need to get off your feet." She called my office from the room, while I was getting dressed.

On the drive home, I called Steven and then Dr. Bonderant. He told me to stay in bed for 24 hours; there was nothing else to do. I had given the "bleeding in early pregnancy talk" hundreds of times. "There is no way to know if you are going to miscarry. This early in pregnancy, there is really nothing to be done. Nothing that you have done caused the bleeding and, unfortunately, there is nothing that you can do to prevent more bleeding or a miscarriage." The only treatment available was bed rest, which might or might not have any effect.

As soon as I had tucked myself into bed, I called the office and talked to Dr. Halle. He said that Dr. Leeds had called and told him that I was bleeding and that she had sent me directly home. He asked how I was, then added, "You know, if you're going to miscarry, you're going to miscarry. Bed rest doesn't really do anything."

Yes, I knew that. I had told hundreds of people that, but I still recommended bed rest.

"Well, Dr. Bonderant advised me to stay in bed," I replied, wondering if Dr. Halle really expected me to show up at work the next day. That sealed my decision; I would get my obstetric care from a different group, at a different hospital. I also felt that, as the only woman in a group of three men, I needed a bit of privacy.

Lying in bed, I picked up the phone and made an appointment with one of the high risk pregnancy or perinatal groups in town. I had interviewed with them and thought they were excellent doctors and delivered excellent care. (They had offered me a position, but Dr. Walker had offered me more money. How could I have missed his abusive, alcoholic personality? Looking back, he had practically attacked Steven on several issues at our interview dinner, well beyond jovial political disagreement.)

The next day, I had an ultrasound at Dr. Bonderant's office. I had not bled overnight, so I was not nearly as worried as I was at Dr. Leeds office. Waiting patiently for my ultrasound, I knew that I had at least grown eggs and gotten pregnant, many steps ahead of most of the women in business suits in the waiting room, looking anxiously at their watches. Not only was I off of work for the day, I was full of estrogen, which gave me a wonderful sense of calm (and a bit of nausea.) I didn't see my friend who had not grown eggs for three cycles. Sitting in the exam room, I remembered how lucky I was to have even gotten pregnant, and vowed that I would do whatever it took to keep my babies.

With an uncharacteristic calmness, I almost floated to the ultrasound room when my name was called. Alone in the dim ultrasound room with just the buzz of the machine, taking off a pair of Steven's blue jeans which I had cuffed at the bottom and were the only pants in the house that fit me now, a more realistic fear overcame me. I might be back in that waiting room on a regular basis. Lots of women got this far, or farther, and lost their baby or babies. I shouldn't have been so greedy and wanted two. Maybe I could only carry one, and now I might lose them both.

Finally, the door quietly opened and the ultrasound tech came in in her pressed scrubs. "Let's see what we have here," she said confidently, squirting warm bluish jelly on my belly. In a quick flick of her wrist, we saw two heart beats. Two heart beats and no more bleeding. She told me to go home to bed, and wait for the nurse to call me.

Enjoying a quiet day in bed, I wondered how long I would have to lie there. One episode of bleeding shouldn't put me out for the rest of the pregnancy. Elizabeth called, and in her charming English accent, told me that everything looked good, and that Dr. Bondurant was releasing me to my obstetrician. "Send us pictures of the babies," she added.

At my first visit to my obstetrician, Dr. Clyde, a woman accustomed to being the doctor's doctor, she made it clear that I was to be the patient. She was to be my police woman and not let me overdo it. Dr. Clyde was in her late 40's, a matter-of-fact but warm woman with glasses, straight brown hair hanging neatly to her shoulders and no make-up. I could easily picture her in a police uniform.

She reviewed how often I would come to the office and how often I would have ultrasounds. She even made sure that I was taking my prenatal vitamins. When she brought it up, I told her that I didn't want an amniocentesis. I didn't want to know if something was wrong with just one baby and make a decision that might cause me to lose both. This was where going through all of that infertility torture paid off. There was no question in my mind about putting these babies at any risk. A 1 in 200 risk of loss or complication per procedure, and I would need two procedures, one for each baby, was too high for me. Dr. Clyde's furrowed thick, brown, unplucked eyebrows seemed to show a little disappointmet at my lack of desire for knowledge in that area, but I simply was not taking any risks. And, I would have plenty of ultrasounds, so, it would be unlikely for the babies to have some horrible anomaly that we didn't find.

Dr. Clyde laid down the law: at 20 weeks I should stop taking call and by 28 weeks, I would probably be on bedrest. Wow. That was not going to be popular in my office. She volunteered to tell my partners, but I declined her offer; I was a big girl. I would tell them myself.

What could they say? Doctors orders. Dr. Walker quickly came up with an alternative plan. Instead of taking call, he assigned me the nurse's job of taking first call on the weekends. That would make the rest of the calls easier for those who were doing the physical labor in the hospital and he could save money by not paying the nurse on the weekends. I handled requests for antibiotics for ear and urinary tract infections, requests for birth control pills from women who suddenly found themselves out of birth control pills and could not possibly wait until the office opened on Monday to get a new prescription, in short, anyone who did not need to come into the hospital. I also talked to the people who did need to go to the hospital, and then called the on-call doctor to let him know. The calls kept me up all night and interrupted any rest that I tried to get during the day all weekend long.

One night, around 18 weeks, while I was still working and taking call, I had a night full of emergencies. After performing a forceps delivery for fetal distress, followed almost immediately by an emergency C-section, my adrenaline had been pumping hard and fast for quite some time. I could not imagine that was good for the blood flow to my uterus. After several hours of non-stop potential disasters, all of my patients and their babies were fine, but I was worried about *my* babies figuring out that this was what my life was like, and deciding that they had not picked a good body after all. Fortunately, I had to call in Pat, the ultrasound technician for the next patient. Pat lived 45 minutes from the hospital, way out in the country. She had six children, and always seemed totally unflappable. I guess nothing in the hospital seemed like much after six children. As I walked out of the room with her after she had scanned my patient, she asked if I was all right.

"I know it's foolish," I began. "I tell patients all the time that stress isn't dangerous for their babies, but I have had quite a night, and I just can't imagine my little ones are okay in there."

In her very motherly voice, she offered, "Let's just slip into one of the empty rooms and take a peak."

I tried to breathe calmly as I lay on the bed in one of the labor rooms, pulling the top of my scrubs up so she could squeeze cold jelly onto my belly. It seemed to take forever for the probe be reactivated and the lights to flicker on the monitor. After several eternities all the right lights were flickering and she put the smooth probe on the white mound that my belly had become. I squeezed my eyes shut, unable to watch while Pat looked for the heart beats.

"They look great," Pat said after only a few very long moments, smiling kindly, showing teeth that had nursed six babies. "You can look, now."

My babies were moving and happy, hearts beating away, enjoying all the excitement, laughing at mommy for worrying.

The next day, I felt as if I might be contracting. Sitting on a black wheeley stool in the operating room, just after my patient had been put to sleep for surgery, I called Dr. Clyde's office to ask if I could come in to be monitored. "Certainly, come on in," the receptionist offered without hesitation.

"Can I come in the afternoon?" I asked. "I'm just about to start a laparoscopy."

"You doctors!" she laughed. "Come as soon as you can."

I tried to think peaceful thoughts, imagining a flat line on a uterine monitor, showing that my uterus was not contracting. The laparoscopy went well. Once I got started, I was more worried about fitting my pregnant belly next to the operating table than about my contractions. My arms were still long enough to reach over my belly. After the surgery, I spoke to the patient's family, dictated my notes of the procedure, changed out of my O.R. scrubs and headed to Dr. Clyde's office. By then, I was no longer contracting. That was great with me. No contractions. My cervix was still fine, long and closed in medical parlance. All systems go.

At 24 weeks, Dr. Clyde put me on home bed rest. At 26 weeks, Dr. Halle and Dr. Walker had the office manager call me at home to come in for a meeting. I can't remember who in the office let me know ahead of time that it might not be a pleasant meeting, that they were going to fire me. I talked over a brief strategy with my husband, talking to him on my cell phone while driving, somewhat shakily, to the meeting.

We all sat on comfortable swivel chairs in the conference room. The newest of the three doctors, the one whose wife had been through IVF, looked a bit embarrassed and seemed to be trying to shrink into the couch. As the new guy, he had been assigned the bad guy role. The upshot was they thought that I should stay at home with my babies. None of their wives worked and they just did not see how having twins would fit into an OB/GYN lifestyle.

I nodded, maintaining my composure, wondering if this were really the late 20th century in the United States of America. Yes, but we were in the very recently rural, now suburban South.

Dr. Walker took over, with the business details. This time, he was not scream-ing, but trying to be very nice, as nice as you can be firing a well-educated, hard-working, intelligent woman who is 26 weeks pregnant with twins. My con-tract provided for three months severance notice, and they would therefore con-tinue to pay me for the next three months, including my production bonus and the raise due at the end of the first year, which would be my last paid month. The insurance coverage would continue through the end of my pregnancy, and then I could go on a COBRA, if I did not want to go on my husband's insurance.

I asked if they would give me good references. Always practical, Steven had reminded me that this would be important.

"Oh, certainly," they all chorused. Each of them could not get a word in soon enough to assure me that they thought I was an excellent doctor.

Did they fire me because I had stayed home the day I bled? Was it because I had gone on bed rest when my doctor told me to? Was it because I had chosen to have different doctors take care of me and that was embarrassing to them as a group? Or was it because they were just assholes? Giving them the benefit of the doubt, I chose the latter.

No one had offered to hold my position at no pay while I was out. That would have seemed reasonable. Given the time of year, they were not going to find a replacement until after I would be back from maternity leave.

I was quite shaken and Steven consoled me on my cell phone the whole way home. It was not the sort of thing to tell a pregnant woman and then expect her to drive safely. But, OB/GYN training teaches you to focus on the task at hand, not to let your own emotions get in the way. I thought about the night my mother-in-law passed away. I was on call. The other residents and even the attending offered to cover for me. Since Steven wanted to be alone with his fam-ily, there was no point in my leaving. I took a few moments to cry, then put my blinders on and focused on my patients. Now, my job was to get my babies and me safely back to the house, up the stairs and into bed.

On the drive home, I looked nostalgically at this landscape. Where farms and forests had been when I visited for an interview just last year, huge tractors were leveling the land and building car dealerships and strip malls. There was a locally owned, run down motel, that would do well to be bought out by Motel 6, and a bar called The Country Club, as in country music, where one of my patients was a bar tender. A cute, young blond who probably did very well as a bartender, she had chosen me as her gynecologist because of the good things she had heard about me from the guys at the bar; they had been impressed with me during their wives' deliveries. Applebee's, Ruby Tuesdays and Hooters provided the gourmet fare along the route.

The next day was Saturday. On the way to the office to reclaim my pictures and books, my husband and I stopped for lunch at the Ruby Tuesday. One of the nurses was having lunch at a nearby table. We chatted, but I didn't mention my conversation with the other doctors. It just didn't come up and didn't seem to flow naturally into the conversation. She didn't seem to know.

CHAPTER 13

▼

DAYS, WEEKS, HOPEFULLY MONTHS

One week after becoming unemployed, Steven drove me to my routine follow-up appointment. I barely fit into the car.

The ultrasound at Dr. Clyde's office showed that my cervix was funneling, that the inner part of my cervix, the part that was supposed to hold the babies in, was weak, allowing the amniotic sac to bulge through. The outside of my cervix, however, was still closed.

Without any fuss, Dr. Clyde instructed her nurse to hook me up to a monitor in another room. With three brown, flat monitor heads (one to measure each baby's heart rate, and one to monitor contractions) pressed against my belly by long white elastic bands, I lay on the exam table and watched the monitor pen marking my fate on a running sheet of white paper with the red grid. Although I didn't feel anything, the pen made big, round, bell-curved humps every three minutes, indicating that I was contracting.

Dr. Clyde knocked and walked in with her business-like gait. She ran the long thin monitor strip through her fingers, nodding her head. "You're contracting," she said.

"I guess so. I haven't felt any of it," I answered.

"Let's get you to the hospital," she said, as she pressed a button on the wall. In a moment, a nurse appeared with a wheelchair. Obediently, I sat in the wheelchair, fumbling with the foot rests. They were truly awkward things.

Steven was worried. I was not. I told him that I sent people to the hospital all the time for these little contractions, and that I would probably go home later that afternoon or evening. The contractions just looked big on the monitor because my uterus was big and I was thin.

The nurse wheeled me into a double room that had only one bed. The sheets were impressively starched and tucked tightly under the mattress. Steven had to pull them out for me so that I could get into the bed after putting on my hospital gown, an elegant beige with a blue diamond pattern.

A few moments later, a seasoned, matter-of-fact nurse, whom you would not dare tease about her big hair, marched into the room, clearly her territory, introduced herself as Eliza, deftly strapped the monitor belts around me, finding each baby on the first try, and gave me an injection of terbutaline, a medicine used for asthma that relaxes smooth muscles, such as the uterus. The injection is with a tiny needle just under the skin. After all the big needles of the progesterone in oil, I thought the tiny needle with only 0.2 mg in the syringe would be a breeze, but it still stung. In addition to relaxing the uterus, terbutaline stimulates your heart to beat much faster, and, it seemed to me, harder. Following Eliza's commands, I drank water and tried to relax. Taking slow deep breaths, I listened to my heart pound.

When the contractions did not stop, Eliza gave me two more doses of terbutaline and started an I.V. to give me more fluids. Dehydration caused the release of a hormone closely related to the hormone oxytocin which women release in labor to cause contractions. Hydration, making sure you had enough fluids, was the first line of defense against preterm labor.

While Eliza was starting the I.V., she sent Steven out to deal with registration forms. Eliza was quick with the i.v, but Steven was gone for, what seemed to me to be, quite some time. He reported that it was nerve wracking in the registration area; he was certain that some of the women were going to deliver before it was their turn to register. "I was afraid I might have to do a delivery," he joked. "Head down, check for a cord around the neck. Isn't that right?"

"The clerk," he continued, "must have nerves of steel. No matter how hard a woman was breathing with her contractions, she just called people in the order they had arrived." That was a blessing. Otherwise, Steven would have let everyone ahead of him and would still be waiting to register.

My contractions slowed down, and, when my heart rate came back down below 120 beats per minute, Eliza gave me terbutaline in pill form.

"Do you think I'll go home tonight?" I asked.

"Not tonight," Eliza answered with conviction. "Maybe tomorrow, if your uterus stays quiet."

The next night, Saturday night, I started contracting again. I buzzed the nurse and asked over the intercom if she could come and check my cervix.

A few minutes later, Dr. Sims, one of Dr. Clyde's partners, appeared.

"You didn't have to come in," I said, apologetically. "It's 11:30 at night. I was happy to have a nurse check me."

She had just picked up her own twins from a party and dropped them off at home when the nurse had called her to say that I was contracting.

I told her that my ex-partners didn't think you could be an OB/GYN and mother of twins. She assured me that it could be done, and named a few other OB/GYN mothers of twins, all with successful practices. "But, for now," she said, "less is more. The less you do the better." She had also been on bed rest, and, at the time, the practice had just been Dr. Sesson, the male senior partner in her now large group, and herself. He had toughed it out, basically running a one person practice, on call all the time, until she had come back to work. A true gentleman.

With firm, gentle fingers, Dr. Sims checked my cervix. It was still closed, but short. She ordered my terbutaline doses to be closer together.

I asked if I could have a Foley catheter in my bladder, so that I wouldn't have to get up constantly. Just walking to the bathroom made my uterus contract.

On Saturday afternoon, before my night of contractions, Eliza had predicted that we would definitely be in the hospital through the weekend. The nurse on Sunday guessed that we would probably be there for the duration, until delivery.

Monday morning, Dr. Sesson, who, 11 years ago, had seen Dr. Sims through her twin pregnancy and bed rest, was on call. He remembered me from my interview a year ago. "Clearly, you made a mistake," he joked. Word had spread through the group of my sudden state of unemployment.

"Now, what are you doing?" he asked, laughing. He had a full head of silvery gray hair and a sparkle in his blue eyes. For his age, which I guessed to be close to 60, he looked quite fit. I remembered that he played a lot of tennis.

I was trying to eat my breakfast in Trendelenberg, a position with my head down and feet up, to reduce pressure on the cervix. It had been my own idea. The hospital bed had all the controls, and I had simply raised the feet and lowered the head.

"At least sit up to eat, or you'll get horrible indigestion," he said, jovially. "We usually only put people in Trendelenberg when the cervix is significantly dilated. Even then, they don't always get a Foley."

"I know," I said, "but it makes me feel like I'm doing something."

"Yes, giving yourself an ulcer and a urinary tract infection. Please, at least sit up to eat."

I pressed the button to raise the head of the bed and thought that it was a shame that this wonderful doctor wanted to retire. Well, he had put in his time.

Later that morning, I called the agency on employment discrimination. I had 180 days from the date of the event to bring a lawsuit. The voice at the end of the phone insisted that I had to appear in person to pick up the forms and file the complaint. Appearing in person did not really seem compatible with hospital bed rest. By the 180 day mark, I should have delivered. I would bring the babies in their stroller. It might even be their first outing. How lovely.

I called Steven at the office to report that I would have to go in person to file a discrimination claim, and added, indignantly, that having to appear in person was further discrimination against pregnant women. In his calm, soothing voice, he reminded me, yet again, that I did not have any financial damages. I had no lost income. My insurance was continuing.

From my hospital bedside telephone, I talked to my women doctor friends and my college roommates. They were all outraged. They all agreed that I should sue.

Steven just wanted me to calm down and not contract. "You can sue if you want," he placated me, "but it will just be to make you feel better. It'll be expensive and you won't get any money from them. They were very smart to give you those three months salary. You will just be giving your money away to lawyers."

Well, that got me. At least for the moment. I certainly did not want to give my money away to lawyers.

That night, Dr. Clyde stopped by, in an evening gown. Standing in the doorway of my dark room, with the hall light behind her, her hair swept up on her head, she looked like a mother come to check on her child after a night out. Laughing conspiratorially, she told me that she had seen Dr. Walker and Dr. Halle at the annual OB/GYN dinner dance; they had asked her to send me a hug and a kiss.

"Excuse me," I said, incredulously. "You can keep the hug and kiss," I answered, wishing she had kicked them in the nuts for me, but that didn't seem the professional thing to say.

"I thought you would be amused," she replied, as if she knew what I was thinking about the nuts.

That weekend, my mother flew down. Steven had stayed in a cot next to me every night, but Mom offered to stay and let him get a decent night's sleep. The nurses were more worried about Steven than about me. Eliza questioned him every time she saw him about his diet. She offered to bake him a casserole.

With my mother lying in the cot next to me, in the darkness of the hospital, I finally cried. I was terrified. I didn't want to deliver 27 week twins. They could bleed into their brains (intraventricular hemorrhage), have their intestines give out (necrotizing enterocolitis), have cerebral palsy, or have horrible asthma if I couldn't hold them in. I felt so helpless.

After my little cry, I put myself on the monitor. Sure enough, my little cry had made me contract. I called whatever nurse answered my call button and I requested some more terbutaline. The voice said that she would come check my Foley. I knew that she was stalling, and didn't want to call the doctor in the middle of the night to get the order for more terbutaline. What was checking my Foley going to tell her?

Since the contractions weren't hurting and I knew that relaxation was the best thing, I willed myself to sleep.

Monday morning, I met Dr. Patton. Poor guy. It was his first day on the job, and there was me, patient from Hell, a panicking OB/GYN, 27 weeks pregnant with twins, and a lawyer husband. It didn't get much worse than that. With short, curly brown hair, energetic eyes and an easy smile, he couldn't have looked much younger. Under his white coat, he wore khaki pants and a polo shirt with a tie.

He had barely finished introducing himself before I started with my request of the day. Since I was still having contractions on the terbutaline, I wanted to be started on magnesium sulfate, an intravenous medication that always makes everyone feel terrible, very hot and sometimes groggy, but is very effective at stopping contractions. One of the side effects of terbutaline is to make you short of breath, so as I requested the magnesium sulfate, I sounded as if I had just run a marathon without any training.

Dr. Patton, fresh and eager on his first day after fellowship, and apparently without enough money to buy a proper suit, patiently explained that if I went on magnesium sulfate, with my heart racing as fast as it was from the terbutaline, I might go into pulmonary edema, a condition of fluid on the lungs, which can be fatal. If my lungs filled with fluid, we would have to stop all the medicine and the contractions might become full blown labor. Instead of killing myself with magnesium sulfate, he suggested transfering me to a terbutaline pump, which would give me a steady dose of terbutaline, with intermittent bolus doses. That was great! From my point of view, having a pump meant that if I needed more in the middle of the night, I didn't have to ask a nurse to ask one of my doctors. I could just give myself an extra dose. The pump, a tiny gray machine that I pinned to my hospital gown, however, did have a preprogrammed limit, so people like me couldn't kill themselves, trying to save their babies.

Dr. Patton also convinced me to get rid of my Foley catheter. He argued that it might cause an infection which would stimulate preterm labor. In addition, he promised to write an order for me to get a bedside commode, so that I would not have to walk all the way to the bathroom. After the first night of contractions, I had lost bathroom privileges and had been taking sponge baths in bed. Having my hair washed depended on a combination of my nurses' moods and how many patients they were assigned. Eliza usually managed to wash my hair every other shift that she had me. With army-like precision, she rearranged the furniture in the room and swung the huge bed into position so that my head could go under the faucet, or at least over the sink.

Dr. Patton suggested that the neonatologist come by to talk to us about what would happen if our babies were born now. Not only were they not going to be born now, I thought that neonatology talk would scare Steven to death. With Steven in mind, I politely declined. When Steven returned that night, he had already been on a NICU tour.

Later that afternoon, Ada, a nurse from the terbutaline pump company came to teach me how to use the magical little box. There was a tiny, but nasty, needle that I had to jab into my thigh. The needle had to go into fat. If it went into muscle, it would hurt a lot, and not work correctly, an undesirable combination. For better or worse, now mostly for the worse, I didn't have much fat. Ada, one of the few nurses not on television that I have seen in a white nurse's uniform, stabbed the needle in, and taped it down. It really hurt. Maybe, I was just a wimp. Ada proceeded to explain which tiny buttons to push to set the machine and how to give myself an additional bolus. Little did she know how often I intended to use that information, I thought.

But, Ada was not born yesterday and she set the machine so that I could only give myself one additional bolus per four hour period. The machine would automatically give me a bolus every four hours, along with a continuous basal dose. I tried hard to concentrate over the pain, which Ada assured me, in her almost masculine voice, was not pain, just some discomfort, and that I would get used to it quickly.

Ada was just standing to leave when the gray machine started beeping. After a thorough inspection, which I tried to follow in hopes that I could figure out how to give myself extra boluses, we discovered that everything was hooked up correctly, but that the medicine wasn't flowing in correctly. The nasty little needle was, in fact, in my muscle. "You need to eat more," she said, as she pinched my thigh, in search of fat.

A few needle stabs later, I was properly set up and Ada walked out, her thick, rubber soled, white nursing shoes not making a sound. The cartridge in the pump ran out at about 4 a.m., causing the gray machine to make a most annoying and continuous beep.

When I called out, the night nurse told me over the speaker that she didn't know how to replace it. The company nurses handled that, but only during regular working hours. Forced into action, I pretended to remember and, somehow, managed, from my clumsy position in the bed, with my swollen pregnant fingers, shaking from the terbutaline, to properly insert the new cartridge.

Terbutaline sped up my already impressive metabolism. The twins took up all of my belly, squishing my stomach. I basically had to eat all day. The hospital nutritionist advised me to drink two milk shakes every day. Steven called every morning around ten to make sure that I drank my hospital milk shake. The hospital milk shake was simply disgusting, a real waste of calories. I made Steven stay on the phone while I drank it.

All day I looked forward to my afternoon milkshake. My friend Samantha worked at and lived near the hospital. Every day, after work, she brought me a milk shake from Baskin-Robbins. As I would slurp down the last delicious drops every evening, she would joke about the guy behind the counter asking her where she was putting all of those milkshakes, and that he must think that she was there to see him. After all, what grown-up woman gets a vanilla milk shake every day?

My college roommate sent me a care package of fattening cheese, cheese crackers and chocolate.

Almost daily, friends or relatives called and asked how I could stand just lying there, doing nothing. Let me assure you that I did not find this helpful. In fact, it seemed to me, modern etiquette should dictate certain things *not* to say to people on bed rest, the first being "How can you stand it?" I had to stand it. And then, there was the word stand. Standing sounded wonderful, after weeks of lying in bed, tossing from one sore hip to another.

Since everyone who called asked how I could stand it, I had a standard reply: I was just having a terrible time, drinking milk shakes, eating steaks and chocolate, reading wonderful books and watching trash television.

The bedside commode was another issue. That was less likely to inspire envy, so, in general, I didn't mention it. Steven stayed with me every night, in the oh-so-comfortable, narrow, beige, vinyl pull-our chair. I didn't think that you should have to see or hear your lovely bride on a bedside commode until you were in your 80's or 90's, and your children had moved you into a nursing home. As with everything, Steven was a good sport. Sometimes, though, if he was awake, I made him get out of bed and wait in the hallway.

Since Steven lost more weight than I gained, the nurses and I tried to convince him to eat some of my cheese and crackers. He refused, not wanting to take food out of his unborn children's bellies.

In the evening, Steven and I started reading to the babies and playing Mozart. We laughed at ourselves. We almost relaxed. One night, I convinced Steven to snuggle with me in the hospital bed, but there really wasn't room for the four of us.

One day, after I complained about my terribly sore hips, my doctors upgraded me to a fancy new air mattress. Very special patient that I was, I was the first one in the hospital to have one. Eliza washed my hair that morning, in honor of the special event. Later that afternoon, just as one shift ended and another began, nurses began to gather in my room. The inflate-a-bed company representative, wearing a brown polyester suit and reminding me of my driver's ed teacher, gave an in-service to the nurses in my room. The bed had controls to adjust the inflation pressure in different parts of the bed. As I lay in the bed, elegant with my newly cleaned hair and my gray hospital gown with a blue diamond pattern, the sales representative deflated and inflated various sections of my mattress. It was as close to an amusement park as I was going to get that summer, and I thoroughly enjoyed it.

Another great feature of the bed, the salesman highlighted, was the gortex sheets. Lying in bed all day growing twins was a very sweaty affair and, for some reason, the gortex sheets didn't make you sweat the way regular sheets did. I loved the blue gortex sheets, but they upset my nurses because my bed never looked "made." You couldn't tuck in "hospital corners" with gortex sheets.

One night, watching the evening news, I saw a report that a few women had died while on the terbutaline pump. Great. "Please don't let my mother hear this," I hoped throughout the news story. No such luck. Within minutes, the telephone rang.

"Did you know that you could die from terbutaline?" my mother asked, genuinely worried, across the miles.

"Mom," I began, in my exasperated daughter voice. "I am in the hospital. One of my nurses used to work in the coronary care unit. I am young and healthy. It is highly unlikely that I am going to die from a medicine that I have been on for several weeks." The words rushed from my mouth, the argument having formulated in my mind the moment I heard the teaser for the upcoming story about "deaths from terbutaline." I didn't mention all of the extra boluses that I gave myself, even if my heart rate was already above 120, the maximum allowed for terbutaline. I didn't mention that I barely slept at night because the medicine made me so jittery. And, I certainly didn't mention that I had received a shot of morphine, a respiratory depressant, the other night when I had used all of the boluses that my terbutaline pump allowed, and was still contracting. Fast heart and slow lungs were a good way to win a trip to the intensive care unit.

"Maybe you should stop taking the medicine," she ventured.

"And have the babies now, no way," I said. Then, because I just had to tease her, I continued, "I won't die suddenly. They should have time for an emergency post-mortem C-section. They should be able to get the babies out in two or three minutes."

By now, Steven, who was sitting next to me, was looking worried, too.

What party-poopers and worry-warts! This was the most fun I had had in weeks, getting everyone all in a dither.

Days went by. Weeks went by. Every Thursday, I got a steroid injection to help the babies mature, in case they came early. Every Saturday, there was spaghetti and meat sauce for dinner. Every day for lunch, I ate a tasteless turkey sandwich on white bread that was dyed brown so that it could be called whole wheat. It was still hard to find fat for the terbutaline needle. My hips got sorer. My belly got bigger. The nights got longer. The days got longer. Steven got thinner.

Samantha organized a baby shower for me in my room. The morning before the party, I changed out of my hospital gown into one of my pretty maternity dresses that was languishing in the closet. Samantha and my mother hung decorations and brought in fancy hors d'oevres. My friends arrived and sat in a horseshoe arrangement, facing me, lying on the bed, like a princess, like the captive princess Aida, trying to free her people from captivity. I envied the busy tension in the room as my doctor friends tried to relax for a few minutes, before hurrying off to see their patients. Most of them worked at the hospital and were wearing casual suits, stopping by in the middle of making weekend, morning rounds.

I tried to open my presents. Even that pathetic effort made me contract, so my mother opened them for me, while Samantha kept the list. Steven insisted that I wear the uterine monitor for the baby shower. The lumps from round, beige monitors looked lovely pressed against my gigantic belly under the red flower print on my white cotton dress. It had not been easy to convince Steven that the effort to put on a nice dress instead of my hospital gown would not cause me to deliver immediately. In fact, he really wanted to cancel the shower. The whole idea terrified him. He said that he would buy me everything that people would bring. I explained to him that the shower was not about the presents. The presents were merely a way for people to show support and to celebrate the new baby. I felt that after all that I had been through, I deserved a bit of celebration. In fact, all women brave enough to get pregnant deserved a celebration. It was society saying that they were glad you were having this baby, even if cost you your job.

Midway through the presents, I had to have everyone step into the hall for a moment while I used my bedside commode. How charming. But, they were almost all doctors. Except for Steven, whose eyes were glued to the uterine monitor, they were all women, which meant that they understood the constraints of small bladders.

While everyone was out of the room, I flipped my monitor upside down so that it wouldn't pick up contractions. I was only worried about contractions that I could feel, but I couldn't convince Steven of this.

Both Steven and I made it uneventfully through the shower. While Mom and Samantha were cleaning up, I asked them to leave the decorations. The pink cardboard storks hanging from the ceiling added a festive air to the otherwise 100% drab room.

Most days just dragged on and on. For almost two weeks, fourteen long days, I tried reading novels, real literature. Every five minutes I checked the clock. While the years had gone too fast, the minutes were now almost at a standstill. Finally, I asked Steven to bring me a Cosmopolitan magazine.

"Won't all that smut make you contract?" he asked, earnestly, his eyebrows furrowed with worry.

"I'll stay on the monitor," I promised. The Cosmopolitan day was a good day; the clock moved quickly. Before I knew it, it was 5 p.m., and almost time for Steven to get "home."

I started watching "Roseanne" twice a day. The news really got on my nerves; there were too many traffic reports, especially for those of us not going anywhere.

Eventually, my doctors started encouraging me to get out a bit, to go for a wheelchair ride. "No," I said, I had seen plenty of hospitals. I had even seen this hospital when I was interviewing.

I held out against the wheelchair ride until the babies were 35 weeks and 4 days gestational age. Finally, I let the nurse take me on a wheelchair ride, just to show me where the Labor Room was in relationship to the operating room. My babies were in a position that allowed me to choose whether I wanted to attempt a vaginal delivery or to have a C-Section. The first baby was head down and the second was lying crosswise, transverse, and would probably be pulled out feet first. I was terrified of labor. I had seen too many simple, healthy labors quickly go wrong. Was I really going to risk something happening to my babies? But, there were benefits to being born vaginally. Coming through the birth canal squeezed fluid out of the lungs so that the newborn could breath. And, I, the mother, would be able to walk the next day, or so I thought.

The labor room for twins was right next to the operating room. If I watched the monitor carefully, I could make sure that I was in the O.R. before anything happened to my babies. Over and over, I envisioned doing my own C-Section, certain that my babies would have fetal distress and my doctor would not arrive quickly enough. Squeezing my eyes closed, I would collect my inner strength to cut through the layers of my own skin, even if I had not yet gotten my epidural. Mind over body. Ignore the pain. Focus on the babies. I only wished that I had a scalpel in the drawer next to my bed. I had my imaginary limits; I wouldn't use the blunt, serrated knife from my food tray, it had to be a proper scalpel.

That night, the night after my wheelchair ride, I started contracting. The next morning, my doctor checked me and sent me to labor and delivery. I was allowed to walk the hallways as my labor progressed. Nothing like trying to walk in labor when you haven't walked for eight weeks. I was also much bigger than the last time I had walked farther than my bedside commode. Around lunch time, one of the doctors came by and broke my water. I was 4 to 5 centimeters dilated. I always told my patients that the contractions got stronger after the water broke or was broken. Boy, I wasn't kidding! YOUCH! Within minutes, I proclaimed that I was ready for the anesthesiologist to give me my epidural. More than ready. Where the hell was he? These contractions really hurt. Poor Steven looked distraught. We had watched a labor video the night before, but he had had no proper birthing class to prepare him. I tried to pretend I was fine, but my cursing with each contraction gave me away.

Finally, I got my epidural. (Probably only a few minutes elapsed. I had been very patient for eight weeks trying to avoid labor, but now that real labor was here, patience was no longer on my list.)

After the epidural, I fell asleep, nice, painless sleep. No sore hips. No racing heart. Around 2:30 in the afternoon, Dr. Chesel, one of the junior associates, someone at my level, a tall brunette with a serious face and glasses, woke me up to check my cervix. She announced that I was completely dilated. I knew that she wanted to go back to the office. I wanted to go back to my nap. "I can't feel anything from the epidural," I said. "I don't think I could push now."

I could see the relief in her eyes. She probably had an afternoon full of patients, and a twin delivery starting at 2:30 would mess up everything. She went back to the office and I went back to sleep.

At the end of office hours, she came back to check me and had me push once. "Stop," she said quickly. "We need to go to the delivery room. The head is right there."

As my labor nurse wheeled me in my hospital bed across the hall, Steven held my hand. Once set up in the room, Steven said, "This is hardly a quiet home birth." Quite a cast of characters filled the room; my labor nurse, a scrub tech ready to go in case of an emergency C-section, an anesthesiologist and nurse anesthetist for the same reason, Dr. Chesel to do a routine delivery of baby A, and Dr. Patton, to do a breech extraction of baby B, the ultrasound technician to watch the heart beat and position of the baby B after Baby A came out, two respiratory therapists from the neonatal unit for each baby. I felt safe.

I pushed once and Baby A slithered out. Dr. Chesel suctioned her nose and mouth, clamped her cord, and walked her over to the baby warmer. Dr. Patton, now several months out of his specialty training, stepped in and began rummaging around in my uterus to find Baby B's feet.

"Check for ankles," Steven said, trying to sound like he was joking. He had learned from my training that it is important to feel for ankles, because you can not pull a baby out by the wrists. They don't fit that way,

In a few moments, Dr. Patton pulled out Baby B, feet first.

I just lay on my back, watching Steven in his blue O.R. shower cap and mask, sing to Baby A. They were letting him hold her. That was a good sign. They let me hold her for a second, then took her to the nursery. Since Baby B was quite small, they wanted to take her right to the nursery. "I love you, honey," I called across the room as they wheeled her in an isolette out of the room.

The nursery team encouraged Steven to stay with me. It did not take Dr. Chesel long to sew up my small episiotomy. Steven and I just gazed at each other as she sewed. We were parents. But were our babies okay? Could I have done a better job? Had I already failed them as a mother?

CHAPTER 14

▼

AROUND THE CLOCK

An hour after delivery, I was back in the room where I had been for the last eight weeks. I was exhausted. The nursery called to say that Levine TWIN A was hungry, but needed to stay in the nursery under bilirubin lights. Could she give her a bottle? "Sure," I said, feeling terribly guilty about not going to the nursery to breast feed her. But, I didn't even know how to breast feed. I didn't think I could move right then. Could you breast feed under bilirubin lights? I forgot to ask.

A few hours later, the nurse brought Baby A to me. What a beauty! Dark brown hair, penetrating eyes, soft skin. "She looks just like you," Eliza said, with a softness I had not heard in the last eight weeks. "Such a serious expression."

How could she have known? My entire life, people have told me that I looked serious. Now, my baby, only a few hours old, suffered the same fate. Since we had done IVF, I had spent my pregnancy wondering if these babies were really my children, joking that they might look like Dr. Bonderant. Now, I harbored no doubt that this serious little treasure, weighing in at 5 lb 8 oz., was mine.

Breast feeding was not as easy as it looked at the mall. I had told hundreds or thousands of patients that breast feeding was harder than it looked. Unfortunately, I was right. She didn't seem interested, and I was certain that it was because I had been too lazy to go up to the nursery to feed her earlier. She would never take my breast, I chided myself, trying not to send myself spiraling downward into a postpartum funk. Eventually, Baby A and I worked it out. After the initial struggle, and it was a struggle, she went on to be a "breast only" baby for the next four months.

After Baby A, now named Alice, had fallen peacefully asleep, I reluctantly returned her to the nursery and trekked to the neonatal intensive care unit to see Baby B, now named Anne. I had been in many neonatal intensive care units (NICU's) to check on babies that I had delivered. Whenever I walked through the doors, I always thought, "Please God, let this baby be all right." There was an odd dichotomy between the awesome power of the NICU and the tiny bodies whose lives hung in the balance. The neonatologists played the role of God's ministers on earth and I almost always wanted to get down on my knees and beg them to save the child I had just sent them. But, I generally maintained my composure and simply asked how the baby was doing, was any of the blood work back yet, what tests were planned, and was the baby requiring extra oxygen.

The NICU's at the hospitals where I had worked usually were staffed primarily by one or two neonatologists. This, however, was a huge NICU, with doctors rotating by shift. A clerk at the door directed us to the correct room for Levine Twin B. She was in one of the back rooms. The farther back the baby, the more serious the condition. Anne was not in the farthest room. She was breathing on her own, not requiring a ventilator.

A nurse appeared at the entrance to Anne's room and guided us to her isolette. At 4 lb. 1 oz., she looked tiny to me. I was not comforted by the fact that there were tinier babies around her. I saw only her, her tiny little chest going up and down. I sat down and talked to her through the round opening in the isolette. "It's Mommy, honey," I said. She took a more comfortable breath and opened her eyes to look at me. She recognized me, I was certain. Why had I not come up here sooner, I chastised myself. My poor baby had been here all alone. I put my hand through the hole in the isolette and touched her sweet little hand. Then, I noticed the I.V. taped to a board around her tiny arm. That put me over the edge, and I started to cry, quickly progressing from whimpers to full-blown sobs. She looked at me with her little eyes, letting me know that she was okay, that I should not worry. Such a reassuring look definitely said, "Mommy, please don't cry." That, of course, brought more tears.

The nurse told me it was time to go. When I said goodnight to Anne, she looked at me with doleful eyes, sad that I was leaving.

The next morning, I was visiting the NICU when the neonatologist was making rounds. When I asked how Levine Twin B was doing, he looked at his list and read me his notes. He clearly had no idea who she was. This was very different from the neonatologists at the smaller hospitals where I worked, who could give me a thorough run down on any patient that I asked about when I saw them in the doctor's lunch room. But, this hospital had protocols. Anne would be having an ultrasound of her brain, to check for bleeding. Before she left she would have a hearing test. (I already knew that she could hear because she had recognized my voice.) Her biggest issues at the moment were maintaining her body temperature and eating. Basically, she was progressing well. He read that from his notes.

Anne's nurse was wonderful. She helped me get comfortable changing the tiny diapers. She called the lactation consultant to help me breast feed. Every three hours, Anne had her diapers changed and was fed. I still cried when I saw the I.V.

The second night, Steven and I were watching Anne sleep in her isolette when something started beeping. She was having a severe bradycardia, a slowing down of her heart rate, which could cause lack of blood flow to her brain. Her heart could also just stop and she could die, my sweet little angel. Her nurse and some other support staff arrived within moments. I took Steven's hand and took a few steps back. A hysterical doctor mother was not going to improve the situation. I wanted to shout for a doctor, but I realized that the nurses, not the doctors, routinely dealt with this situation. I held my breath and watched the heart rate monitor, wishing that I did not understand it, that I could just feel comforted because someone had turned off the alarm.

The whole situation did not last for more than five minutes, but scarred me for life. Eventually, the terrible beeping of the alarm stopped and the nurses dispersed, leaving Anne somewhat shaken-looking, but with a normal heart rate. I tried to sound calm and to comfort her. Soon, she fell asleep and we left, realizing that she needed her rest and that we could not do anything more than love her.

Steven and I made a recording of ourselves reading and singing to Anne. We bought a tape recorder with a special pillow amplifier that could be placed in Anne's isolette. In my new mother love and hormonal lack of inhibition, I even sang some lullabies on the tape.

Meanwhile, Alice continued to do well. She was a super little breast feeder. I loved watching those tiny but chubby cheeks go up and down with each suck. She loved to be held and I loved to hold her.

Steven and I attended infant CPR class, memorizing how many puffs per sternal compression, how hard to push with each compression, how many "blows" to the back when the child was choking. I could not imagine doing any of this to my itty bitty babies.

After three days, I was discharged. Somehow, my doctors got an extra day for me. Although I was eager to get out of the hospital after eight weeks, leaving Anne was traumatic.

The nurse wheeled me down the hall, proudly holding Alice. After 8 weeks, all of the nurses knew me, and I waved like a queen as my wheelchair chariot rolled down the hall. Steven pulled up to the hospital exit and we buckled Alice into her new car seat, securing her head so that it would not flop. I sat in the back seat, next to her, to talk to her and to keep her head on straight. She had such eager eyes, taking in so many new things. Shortly, she fell asleep.

When we arrived at the house, my mother and the baby nurse were waiting. Somehow, Steven and my mother had everything set up. Clothing had been bought and washed. Steven had created a personalized home shopping network for me and videoed my choices at the baby store. He had built the cribs and decorated them with bumpers and mobiles. He had bought monitors and bottles and diapers and wipes.

We made it through the first night, but changing the diapers the next morning proved to be too much for us. Somehow, we soiled every onesie that we owned within the first two changes of just one baby.

A nurse came to weigh Alice, and to set us up with special lights for bilirubin. Her level was still a bit high. I knew that high bilirubin caused brain damage. The home "bililights" consisted of a neon wrap, with fluorescent lights arranged like bubble wrap. Alice looked like a space creature, wrapped in that glowing blanket.

After feeding Alice, it was time to head to the hospital for Anne's feeding. I brought some pumped milk in one of the cold carrying bags the formula companies gave to new moms. My doctor told me that I could only make one trip per day. I intended, of course, to ignore her and to drive constantly back and forth from home to the hospital, to be able to feed each baby every three hours. Since I couldn't drive yet, I was at the mercy of my husband and mother, who chose to follow the doctor's orders, presumably for my sake.

Despite rushing as fast as my postpartum body could rush, I arrived at the NICU a few minutes late, but the nurse had waited for me. Great, now my baby had had wet diapers for an extra ten minutes. The nurse also made it clear, that waiting for me this time was a one time exception. The nursery ran on a strict schedule, and next time she would have to feed Anne without me. Anne did not seem to mind the delay and lay patiently while I gently wiped her delicate bottom and changed her tiny diaper. Then the nurse allowed me to hold her and feed her. We tried breast feeding for a few minutes, but, not wanting to use up her precious energy, we moved to the bottle. It felt so good to hold her, to feel her gentle breath against my skin, but I knew too much stimulation wasn't good for her. So, I felt guilty when I held her, and even guiltier when I finally put her down and had to leave.

Back at home, Alice was ready to eat the moment I walked in the door. I raced up the stairs to her as quickly as my post partum, post 8 weeks of bedrest, legs would go, tore open the buttons on my shirt and watched Alice happily nurse. Did Alice know that I had left her? Did Anne feel lonely and abandoned at the hospital? How I longed to be able to be in two places at once. If only I could leave one breast at the hospital.

I was too tired to put up a fuss to go back to the hospital in the evening.

The nurse called with Alice's bilirubin results. They were within the normal range, but the top of the range. She informed me that we no longer needed to use the bilirubin wrap. I was not satisfied with a bilirubin level that was almost too high, but I didn't want to unnecessarily toast my child in an electric blanket. Instead, I took her outside to let the sunshine do its natural work.

Every day, I agonized about leaving Alice and what time would be best for Anne. Should I go in the morning, so she would know that I hadn't forgotten her? Should I go in the evening, so that she had something to look forward to and would sleep well, having just seen her mommy?

Within a few days, Anne was moved to the "feeders and growers room." She no longer needed an I.V. and was eating measurable amounts. She was promoted from a prison-like isolette to an open bassinette. She remained on a strict three hour schedule, left in her bassinette until the three hours were up, unless I came to visit.

Anne came home after nine days, looking even smaller than Alice had, engulfed in the car seat. She remained on a three hour schedule, not bothering to request attention between the assigned times. I didn't think that was healthy. I wanted spunky girls. So, whenever Anne whimpered, I raced to her crib, checked her diaper and offered her milk. Still, she stayed pretty much on a three hour schedule.

Anne continued to need a supplement to breast milk. I bought a capillary tube that attached to a bottle and was taped to the end of my nipple. She didn't particularly like it, and ripping the tape off of the already sore skin around my nipple at the end of each feeding hurt like hell, so we abandoned that.

My life consisted of feeding one baby, feeding the other baby and then pumping, so that there would be breast milk for Anne. By then, it was almost time to start again. My baby nurse held water for me so that I could drink while I breast fed. She tried to keep me talking at night, so that I would not fall asleep and drop whomever I was feeding. I heard ALL about her other families, especially the family with whom she had been for an entire year. I tried to imagine what she would say about us. I thought of myself as so normal and dull, now a good thing, if I was to be the topic of midnight conversations.

I answered the phone by saying "Dairy Queen, may I help you?" and was quite proud of my babies' growth.

Mom was a super trooper, holding babies, changing diapers, and, mostly, making sure that I got fed. There was too much physical work to be done for any mother-daughter spats, and, after becoming a mother myself, I had a new-found tremendous respect for the stupendous accomplishments of conception and carrying a child, neither of which I had done terribly well. What was the most overwhelming sensation, however, was the love that I felt for these babies. Had my mother loved me that much? Did she still love me that much? How could I ever repay that much love? I ate an extra drumstick at dinner when she said that I needed more calories while I was breast feeding.

The first trip to the pediatrician was a major expedition, requiring four adults (two physicians, a professional child care provider and a lawyer), and two overflowing diaper bags packed with cold, stored breast milk, diapers, wipes, changes of clothes, and bibs. The babies were growing well, but I looked so awful that my pediatrician encouraged me to stop breast feeding, or at least to move the babies' feedings further apart.

We went to the pediatrician every week. With each trip, the feedings would move to three to four hours apart because of the time in the car and the office. The babies survived the delay in their feedings quite well, but, gradually, during the following week, the feedings crept closer together until we were back on the two hour plan.

CHAPTER 15

▼

IT'S HARD TO GET GOOD
HELP THESE DAYS

After a month, it was time for my mother and the baby nurse to leave. I had been interviewing nannies and had chosen a nice West African lady to start the day before the baby nurse left. In addition to having a nice manner with the babies, I thought she could teach them French.

I made it very clear to the agency (to whom I paid several hundred dollars for the privilege of interviewing their candidates—it cost several thousand if you hired one) that I needed someone legal, with a social security number and a Green Card or, a U.S. citizen. I made it very clear to my interviewees that I needed someone legal. This woman had come back for a second interview and claimed to have been legal, but did not show up on her first day of work. The only explanation was an inability to produce a Green Card.

Not having a nanny worried Steven, but I was excited about being alone with my babies. We had a wonderful time. We ate and slept and went for walks. I nursed them, took pictures of them and read to them. At two months old, they were a captive audience and loved rhymey baby books. They did not show too much interest in articles in my medical journals, and Danielle Steele novels seemed inappropriate.

Between naps, I interviewed nannies. One woman worked as a hair dresser and had bright green fingernails longer than most talons. When I asked her how she expected to change a diaper with those nails, she replied that she was able to braid hair with no problem. She had not had any actual experience changing a diaper since she had acquired the nails. Despite the pretty sparkle appliqués, those nails were not going anywhere near my babies' precious bottoms.

If applicants asked to hold a baby without washing their hands, they were out. If they did not ask to hold a baby, if they could possibly look at my adorable babies and not be overcome with a burning desire to hold them, they were out.

And the references were wonderful. One little boy, who told me that he was eight years old, volunteered, "Oh, she was a lazy bitch. She just sat in front of the television all day." Whether or not that was true, she clearly had not been a favorite of his. Another woman told me that the day after her son had spent the night at the nanny's house, the nanny's boyfriend had shot the nanny's ear off in that same apartment. I was certain that same boyfriend had been waiting in a car outside my house. Lovely.

I gave the agency that had sent the first seemingly wonderful, but illegal, nanny a second chance. I should have known that it was a bad sign when the woman called from a pay phone twenty minutes after the appointed time of the interview. She was at a Burger King, near a bus stop, about ten minutes from my home, and wanted me to come pick her up. I got both girls strapped into their car seats, attached the car seats into the back of the Toyota Camry and drove to Burger King. The applicant opened the front door, and her friend opened the back door. Upon seeing that the back seat was full of car seats and babies, the applicant offered to hold one of the babies on her lap in the front seat, while her friend sat where the car seat was.

"That's actually against the law," I said, as calmly as I could. "Your friend will have to wait here, if you would like to come to the house for an interview."

My babies remained safely in their car seats, and before we reached the first traffic light, I had ascertained that this woman was nowhere near having a Green Card, although she had heard of one. I turned around and drove her back to Burger King.

When I got home, after unpacking my babies, I called the agency and unsuccessfully tried to get my $200 registration fee back.

The next day, I placed an ad in the paper. First, I studied the ads. There were columns of ads. Some of the ads were half a column, clearly expensive, boasting great accommodations and benefits for the nanny. Private entrance. Private phone line. An entire suite with its own kitchen. A nanny car. What did I have to offer? I had actually been thinking of placing an ad outlining what I wanted in a nanny, rather than what I had for the nanny.

I persevered in my foolhardy desire to place an ad for the nanny that I wanted and wrote out several drafts. "Nanny needed for twins. Eighty hours per week." No, that did not sound right. "Insomniac needed for night-time feedings." Too honest.

What I really wanted was a grandmother to come look after all of us. The very sensitive man taking the advertisement informed me that I was not allowed to advertise for a "grandmotherly" nanny because that was sex discrimination. "Nurturing," however, was acceptable. In the end, with no private suite or nanny car to offer, I had to sell us, and we became the "Nurturing family seeking loving nanny for adorable twin baby girls." After that just came the hard details, "Live-in, non-smoker, driving a plus."

I didn't think that anyone would answer my ad, since we weren't offering a chauffeur and maid service for the nanny. Nonetheless, the helpful gentleman at the paper assured me that I didn't want applicants calling my home phone. On his advice, I set up a voice mail box. That cost a few extra dollars, but we were still way below my husband's suggestion of signing up with a third nanny agency.

Boy, did the calls come in, almost twenty each day. I tried to call back everyone, with a few exceptions. The woman who left a message saying, "I ain't never done nothing like this before, but I needs the money," did not get a call back. However, I did appreciate her honesty.

Then, one day, there was a call, in a beautiful English accent. She left a message that she had been an au pair looking after twins and had always wanted to be a nanny. I could not call her back fast enough. Isabella came for the interview, on time, in her own car. She was married, but did not plan to have children soon. She washed her hands before holding the babies. She held them gently, yet securely. She had worked for Jewish families and knew about not eating pizza on Passover. Her references loved her.

Now, I was worried that she would not pick us. After all, there were columns of ads looking for nannies in the paper.

A few weeks later, Isabella started. The first day, we took the babies for a stroll around the neighborhood. A few hours later, we noticed that Anne's left eye was red. Maybe a leaf had fallen on it or a stray strand from her knit cap had irritated it. Fearing that she would become blind if she did not get immediate attention, I called the children's hospital. The nurse advised me to bring her in to make sure there was no corneal damage. I panicked. My baby was going to be blind.

Isabella didn't think Alice should go to the hospital with Anne. As a strong believer in germs, I agreed. No reason to subject both of them to the incredibly dangerous germs in the hospital waiting room. Steven couldn't get home for a while. That meant that I had to leave my baby with this new woman. She seemed perfectly safe and normal, but so did many psycho-nannies and kidnappers. I left Alice and Isabella in the house and begged Steven to come home as quickly as possible. Isabella was right next to me when I called, so I couldn't tell him it was because I was afraid that this nanny, whom I had chosen, might kidnap Alice, that he might come home to an empty house and we would never see our sweet baby again.

As it turned out, everything was fine. Anne's eye was fine. Alice was asleep when I got home, and Isabella was eagerly waiting to find out what the doctor had to say about Anne's eye.

"What a day," I said to Steven, as I snuggled against his chest for a few hours of sleep before a baby woke up.

CHAPTER 16

▼

BON APPETIT

Once I knew that my babies were safe and secure, I was ready to go back to work. I just needed a job. Now, I was glad that I had not sued my previous partners. One of the nanny interviewees was in the midst of suing a big hotel for what she thought could be work related injuries. I didn't want to be her fall back if the big hotel thing did not work out. I was sure that no one wanted to hire someone suing her last practice. In any case, one day while I was at home peacefully playing with my babies, my last day to file an employment discrimination suit passed.

This time around, I had enough friends to find out about any future employers. I sent out resumes and followed up with phone calls. I was pleasantly surprised by how many groups were looking for another doctor. Within a few weeks, I had several interviews set up. Most people knew my previous employers. They would often say polite things such as, "I don't see you with them." One of my favorite lunchtime comments was, "He was the chief asshole of our class." At least, I felt vindicated.

I spent most of my days in a t-shirt and sweat pants, nursing and changing diapers and reading nonsense, board books. Two days before my first interview, I realized that I didn't have any appropriate interview clothing. None of the zippers or buttons on my interview clothing from two years ago would close. After having been the same size since high school, my body now bulged in new and bizarre places.

Armed with determination and a credit card, I headed to the mall on my first business related venture. I nursed both babies before I left.

The bright mall lights welcomed me back to the joys of retail therapy. The energy of bright colors and 40–60% OFF SALE signs surged through me. I walked quickly toward my favorite department store. When I started trying on suits, I was a size eight. Pretty good for two months post partum. An hour and a half later, still looking for that perfect suit that would make my new figure look like my old figure, my breasts had swollen to a size twelve. They made nursing blouses, but not expanding blouses. The sound of a baby crying would blow me up to a size fourteen.

I finally settled on a Cranberry suit, in a size 12, with a cream colored silk blouse with a paisley pattern. The blouse, also a size 12, masked the lumps of the breast pads pretty well, but if it wasn't too hot, I was definitely going to keep my jacket on. And, I would be saying a prayer that the breast pads worked. Nice round milk stains over the nipples would certainly ruin the professional cache of my new outfit.

My old black shoes would work, but I decided to stop by the shoe department, just in case. As it turned out, my feet were a size bigger. I had always been self-conscious about my feet. One of my friends at summer camp was my height and had shoes three sizes smaller than mine. The fact that this caused her no end of knee and general balance problems didn't make me any less jealous. In fact, I could still picture her cute, little clogs twenty-some years later. She wore a five, and now, I was a ten. Ouch. For consolation, I told myself that this would improve my balance, and I bought an entire new shoe wardrobe.

By now, my breasts were throbbing. I had to get out of the store before I heard another baby cry. With the new suit on a hanger stabbing into my fingers as it hung over my shoulder and the harsh strap of the large shopping bag brimming with shoe boxes digging into my other hand, I hurried to the car.

The keys. Where were my car keys? I draped my new suit gently over the hood of the car and set down the bag of shoes. Then, I began rummaging around in my purse. It had been a while since I had had to do that. They have to be in here somewhere. I had driven here. I had not taken them out of purse. Finally, I kneeled down on the parking lot floor and emptied everything out of my purse, the sounds of my babies at home, screaming in hunger, pounding in my brain. Ah, there they were, at the very bottom.

My first interview was a lunch meeting, at 12:30. I had all morning to get organized. I had planned out the timing of the nursing, of my shower, of getting dressed. When I was all dressed and ready to go, I decided to nurse one last time. Good. No leakage. I readjusted my bra pads and buttoned back up.

By now, with the additional nursing of two babies, I was running on a very tight schedule. I raced to the kitchen to grab a glass of juice. Breakfast had not been part of my plan, and I was feeling a bit light headed. As I swung open the refrigerator door, a bottle of precious, stored breast milk tumbled out and spilled all over my new suit and blouse. My *only* suit and blouse. How could that have happened? Why was the milk in such a precarious position? Why was the top not on tightly? And, why now? This had never happened before. It seemed to me, even if there was no use crying over spilled milk, I deserved to be able to cry over this.

But, there was no time for tears, only for some quick curses. Thank goodness the babies were upstairs and could not hear the four letter words spewing from my mouth. I ran upstairs and rummaged through my wardrobe. I found a silk outfit that I had bought for the rare post-partum night out. It wasn't exactly business attire, but was somewhat formal and didn't have milk stains on the front.

Abandoning any hope for food or drink before the interview, I searched upstairs and downstairs in the house for my purse, then searched the depths of my purse for my keys. Once on the road, I held the directions in front of the steering wheel. It was time for some country western music to settle the nerves, while I drove exactly five miles over the speed limit.

I arrived at the physicians' office exactly two minutes early. The receptionist smiled and told me that all of the doctors were running late. She invited me to have a seat and offered me a cup of coffee. I had to decline. The last thing my frayed nerves and empty stomach needed was a cup of coffee. I took advantage of the time to collect my thoughts. What would they ask me? Usually, it was the age old question, "why did you want to become a doctor?" I had been rehearsing the answer to that question since second grade.

Finally, one of the doctors invited me to the conference room, and we chatted while the others finished seeing patients. She started with the apparently friendly icebreaker, asking if I had children. I volunteered that I had twins, and wanted to add that I was infertile and couldn't have anymore, that she wouldn't need to worry about my taking another maternity leave.

She asked the also apparently harmless question, "Are they identical or fraternal?"

When I answered "fraternal," I hoped that she would guess that they were from IVF. Identical twins are almost always spontaneous, whereas fraternal twins are much more likely to be from some type of fertility treatment.

Eventually, we ended up at Applebee's, a suburban, chain restaurant. I tried to be restrained and not wolf down my water and all of the rolls on the table, since I was starving and dehydrated. As tempting as the full turkey dinner or huge plate of fettuccine looked, I ordered my usual, a grilled chicken salad. It was lady-like and easy to eat, with very little chance of dripping anything, if I didn't use any salad dressing.

I had several more grilled chicken lunches with various groups in various parts of town. If they liked Dr. Walker, they were out. In general, this was not a problem.

My favorite group didn't take me out for lunch. Everyone just stopped by one of the doctor's offices and chatted. I really liked all of them. We set up a dinner appointment with Steven and their spouses. The night before that dinner was the first night the twins slept through the night. I felt giddy with success and a full night's sleep. At dinner, the conversation flowed, and everyone ordered large dinners, the porterhouse steak or the two pound lobster. One of the partners asked the waitress for more rolls. These were my kind of people.

CHAPTER 17

▼

TRUTH TIME

Mrs. Nickels, the office manager, already had my office furnished and decorated when I arrived for work a quick month later. The walls were a rich hunter green, and the elegant desk was my favorite reddish mahogany, with matching chairs upholstered in a red and green fabric. I had chosen a lamp with an equestrian motif that had matching colors and stood lit on the desk. I put down the blotter and pen set which mother had given to me. They matched the desk perfectly. I carefully placed pictures of my adorable babies on the shelves, mindful that they might be painful for my infertility patients, but hoping that, instead, they would be a sign of hope.

Anne and Alice had been asleep when I left that morning. I kissed their sweet faces before I left and threw my breast pump over my shoulder as I headed out the door. Now, I tucked the breast pump under my new desk and looked at my schedule. There might be time to pump at lunch.

The plan was that I would spend most of my day meeting the women who were due to deliver in the next few weeks, so that I would not be a stranger walking into their room for delivery on my first few days of call. There were also a large number of gynecology patients who had been waiting for my arrival to have their annual check-up.

Everyone was so nice: the patients, the office staff, the other doctors.

"We are so glad you're here," I heard throughout the day.

I enjoyed meeting my new patients. They were other doctors, lawyers, home-makers, accountants, executives, business owners, and a few students. They welcomed me warmly.

At lunch, I didn't feel as if I needed to pump. The doctor in the neighboring office, a mother of three, asked how I was doing on my first day away from my babies. I knew that they were happy at home. They had already been drinking formula from a bottle. I had spent a month with the nanny. I knew that she would be reading to them in her beautiful English accent, and telling them stories. They were doing their thing, and I was doing mine.

When I got home, I put Alice to my breast. Nothing. Empty. I was a bit sad, but she simply pulled away and smiled at me with a "time to play, mommy," smile. She was "over it." I put Anne and Alice on my lap and read a rhymey nonsense book. They both smiled and smiled at me as I hugged their tiny bodies and kissed their chubby little cheeks. They knew that mommy loved them.

By the end of the week, I was in the routine of a work *day*, coming home every night. That weekend, however, I was on call. The change in routine started first thing in the morning. I had to be in the hospital, ready for anything, an hour earlier than I usually arrived at the office.

At 7:10 a.m., I was circling the parking deck to my spot, labeled "Dr. Levine." I loved that sign. Something about having a marked parking spot made me feel as if I had "made it." The sign also made me feel as if I belonged. 7:10. For once, I had plenty of time.

As I strode to the hospital building and climbed the steps to the second floor, I admired the light green walls, clean tile floors and lack of smell.

Every door to the delivery floor had a special lock so that no one could escape, kidnapping a baby. Each time I pushed a code, I remembered that other people were still desperate for a child.

I changed into blue scrubs and my blue rubber operating room clogs, pressed some buttons on my pager to make sure that it was on, and walked out to the post partum unit to start rounds.

The first patient, having had a C-section the night before, was putting on her make-up. She asked a few questions about the surgery and recovery, and then we chatted about decorating nurseries. She had had a boy and had a train motif waiting for him in his room at home. I had chosen pastel animals for my daughters.

The next patient was thirty-nine years old. She had four children at home. She had had a quick and easy labor, but then hemorrhaged after the delivery. After so many deliveries, her uterus had not been able to contract normally, to stop the blood flow. Her husband, who had spent the night on the cot next to her, told me how frightened he had been by all of the blood, and how calm my partner and the nurses had been, giving his wife injections to contract her uterus and massaging her uterus to help it to contract. The bleeding had stopped just as they were preparing to take her to the operating room. She had not had much bleeding since that night. Today counted as the second day after delivery, even though she had delivered just before midnight the night before last. Her insurance company would not cover an extra day, so I sent her home with about half of her normal blood count, to care for four children and a newborn. Her husband assured me that his mother-in-law was there to help out. I emphasized that his wife really needed to take it easy. She should not have any more responsibilities than nursing her baby.

My pager beeped. It was Labor and Delivery. I called them back. "We need you for a delivery in Room 10," a voice said urgently.

I headed quickly down the hall, thinking, "I didn't know I had a patient in Room 10."

As it turned out, I didn't have a patient in Room 10. The patient's doctor was in the parking lot, and this was the patient's third baby. It wasn't waiting for anyone. As I scrubbed my hands and donned my delivery gown and gloves, I introduced myself.

"It's coming," the woman shouted from behind her pregnant belly. I gently put my hands around the baby's head and guided it slowly out, to try to avoid tearing the surrounding tissue.

Next, I slipped my index finger down to the baby's neck to check for a cord. The cord was wrapped so tightly around the neck that I could not slip it off. I picked up two clamps to clamp off the cord while it was still around the neck. As I was doing this, I explained to the father what I was doing and that if he had planned to cut the cord, he could help cut it for the belly button with the nursery nurses.

"She had some deep variables," the nurse, whom I had not met yet either, explained. "I thought it was just the rapid descent of the head."

My pulse quickened. How long had this baby had a concerning heart rate tracing? Was I going to be sued as the delivering physician?

I kept working, suctioning out the baby's mouth with a big blue bulb, and easing the baby's body from its mother. The baby screamed vigorously, as I raised it onto its mother's belly. "Is it a boy or a girl?" the contented, happy voice of the new mother asked.

"I didn't even look," I answered. "You tell me," I said, holding the baby up, so that the parents could be the first to see.

"Congratulations!" I heard from behind me. "I missed all of the fun." Their doctor had arrived.

As I stood up to pull off my delivery garb and to relinquish my seat to her physician, I asked, "What's her name?"

"Ashley Tiffany," both parents answered.

"Well, she certainly has started out as an impatient little girl," their doctor said, sitting down to deliver the placenta.

"Good luck. Enjoy your baby," I said, backing out of the room.

I wrote a quick note in her chart and headed back down the hall to continue my rounds.

The next two patients had just delivered, uneventfully, the day before. The one who had a boy wanted to discuss the pros and cons of circumcision. I told her that, from a gynecologist's perspective, the virus that can cause cervical cancer can live in the foreskin. Therefore, for the sake of his future wife, he should be circumcised. Also, circumcised men almost never get penile cancer. But, probably the most important issue was that he should look like his father. I told her that she didn't need to decide this minute, but that it was much simpler for her, if she wanted to have her son circumcised, to have it done before she left the hospital the next day. The other woman had had a girl, and our conversation focused on breast feeding.

The next patient had had a C-Section for twins three days ago. They had been from in vitro fertilization. She knew that I had twins and asked if twins ran in my family.

I hesitated. Nobody in my new world knew that I was infertile. I could start with a new identity. Was it anybody's business if my children were conceived in the heat of passion on a balmy night on some Caribbean island or in a Petri dish in a sterile lab? Did it matter? Yes, it mattered. And it was part of my job, as a leader and doctor to make it okay. There should be no stigma for the mother or the children. If I hid from it, how could I expect my patients to feel comfortable? And, how could I expect the world to welcome this new generation of babies from mothers who were willing to go through so much to have a baby?

I decided on the whole truth. "Yes, my mother's cousin has twins. Twins can be genetic from the mother's side. But, I got mine the same way you got yours. It seems to me now to be part of God's plan. If I hadn't gone through all of that, I wouldn't have my particular wonderful babies. They're so sweet and adorable. They're four months old now, and I have loved every minute. You are going to love being a mother."

"I already do," she answered. "The love is unbelievable."

CHAPTER 18

▼

YEARS LATER

On a bright summer day, Anne and Alice were spinning madly on a tire swing, their long, brunette hair flying behind them, as they shrieked, "Faster Mommy!" with every revolution. It must have reminded them of the prewomb experience, almost nine years ago, when half of their being was a little sperm being spun down in a centrifuge, because no sooner had I slowed the swing and their feet touched the ground, than they had to know how babies were really made. With their beaming sun-bronzed faces, their sun-streaked brown hair mirroring their internal energy, and, glistening hazel eyes which they had inherited from me, they giggled as they demanded to know the awesome details behind the fact that mommies and daddies have babies. They knew there was a boy part and a girl part, and that they met in the mommy's tummy. But, now they wanted to know more of the transportation specifics.

"Where do you think the boy part comes from?" I asked, when they had settled down enough to listen.

Uncharacteristic silence ensued. They stared at me, a bit frightened of what they might hear, but not ready to change the subject.

"What is the grossest place you can think of for it to come from?" I asked, proud of my Socratic method.

"The penis," they squealed in unison.

"Yes," I replied. "The penis goes inside the vagina and the boy parts come out. Then they swim up the vagina into the uterus to meet the girl part."

"That is just awful, Mommy," Alice announced, squishing her face into a grimace.

"I'm going to adopt," Anne declared.

"Did Daddy really put his penis in your vagina?" Alice asked, with the disgust she might have displayed with a crushed animal in the road, innards exposed.

"But, that's not how you got here," I interjected quickly, feeling like the first third grader to get her period, desperately not wanting her friends to be repulsed. "Daddy left his boy parts in a cup. A doctor mixed it with my girl parts, called eggs. Then, he put you back in."

"That's how I want to have my babies," Anne immediately decided.

Just then, Jennifer, their friend from swim team, ran over to us. "Guess what?" Alice announced. "We just found out how babies get made!"

A year older than Anne and Alice, Jennifer proudly answered, "I already know."

"But, that's not how we were made," Alice stated, completely innocently, with no thought that anyone would ever condemn her or tease her for being different.

"So, you're test tube babies?" Jennifer matter-of-factly replied.

"Absolutely," Anne and Alice answered proudly.

978-0-595-36265-3
0-595-36265-6

Printed in the United States
41809LVS00008B/121

9 780595 362653